The Children of the Chapel

The Children of the Chapel

Mary Gordon and
Algernon Charles Swinburne

Edited with an Introduction by

Robert E. Lougy

OHIO UNIVERSITY PRESS: ATHENS

Library of Congress Cataloging in Publication Data

Leith, Disney, Mrs.
  The children of the chapel.

    Originally published: 1864.
    Summary: In the year 1559, ten-year-old
Arthur Savile is impressed into the service of
the Chapel Royal, where he is brutally mistreated
but learns to survive by means of his wit and
ingenuity.
    1. Great Britain. Chapel Royal—Fiction.
2. Great Britain—History—Elizabeth, 1558-1603—
Fiction. [1. Great Britain—History—Elizabeth,
1558-1603—Fiction] I. Swinburne, Algernon
Charles, 1837-1909. II. Lougy, Robert E.
III. Title.

PR4883.L4C5 1982   823'.8 [Fic]   82-6436
ISBN 0-8214-0631-0   AACR2

Acknowledgements

I am grateful to Charles W. Mann, Curator of Penn State's Rare Books Collection, for his assistance and advice and to the Research Office of Penn State's College of Liberal Arts for a grant which made possible the preparation of this manuscript. I would also like to thank my colleagues for their advice and suggestions and especially John D. C. Buck for sharing with me his knowledge of children's literature. Finally, I want to thank the editorial staff of the Ohio University Press for its direction, assistance, and support.

Robert E. Lougy
University Park, Pa.

Contents

Introduction

There have perhaps been stranger collaborations in the history of English fiction than that which led Mary Gordon (later Mrs. Disney Leith) and her cousin, Algernon Charles Swinburne, to write *The Children of the Chapel*, but none comes immediately to mind. For one of the collaborators was a young woman who had previously written only one work, a novel for children.[1] Her values seem to have been at once unambiguous and irreproachable; her religion, Anglican, devout, and conventional. The other was a young man who had already written some of the finest poems of the age. But his religious profession —pagan and outspokenly anti-Christian—and erotic poetry would soon alienate him from much of English society. It was, in fact, his poetry that Thomas Hardy would cite in *Jude the Obscure* when he wished to suggest the intellectual and religious radicalism of Sue Bridehead: "Thou hast conquered, O pale Galilean; the world has grown grey from thy breath;/ We have drunken of things Lethean, and fed on the fulness of death."

And yet there is also a certain appropriateness to their collaboration. They were, after all, cousins, although their relationship was, as Mary Gordon suggested, rather complex:

> Our mothers (daughters of the third Earl of Ashburn-ham) were sisters, our fathers, first cousins. . . . Added to this, our paternal grandmothers, two sisters and co-heiresses—were first cousins to our common grandmother; thus our fathers were also second cousins to their wives before marriage.[2]

This convoluted consanguinity led to a close bond between Mary Gordon and those relatives she referred to as her "Swinburne cousins." Algernon, she writes, "was to me as an elder brother, a loved and sympathetic playmate, as in later years a loyal and affectionate friend" (*PR*, 4). She would outlive Swinburne by seventeen years and would, in her tenacious defense of his reputation and fame, provide evidence of her own loyalty and affection. She was not only a prolific writer, with a number of novels, stories, and translations of Icelandic plays and sagas to her credit, but also a strong-willed woman who must have been gifted with a healthy body and hearty constitution. She was well into her eighties when she died in 1926 and is reported "to have bathed in the Arctic off the shores of Iceland when she was seventy."[3]

In their later years, Mary Gordon and Swinburne kept in touch primarily through correspondence and actually saw little of each other, although they did share in common a few mutual visits to Putney, the Swinburne family home. It is hard to know exactly how familiar Mary Gordon was with Swinburne's later personal life, but at times it seems that she knew more than she really wished to admit, as in her suggestion that "whatever his religious opinions were or not, however much they departed from those of our upbringing—as doubtless they did in later days—I never, in our years of unfettered and familiar intercourse, remember him to have said anything to shock or distress me. . . ." (*PR*, 31). She would maintain to Edmund Gosse that Swinburne was not irreligious, having "been in communion with the Church of England all his life" and also that he "was never intoxicated in all his life" (*Letters*, VI, 237). We have to admire the kind of singlemindedness that permitted her such illusions—if, indeed, they were such—even while we must acknowledge that the image she defended bore little resemblance to the more commonly held perception of Swinburne.

The Swinburne that Mary Gordon defended throughout her life was the cousin she remembered from her girlhood days when they used to walk together over the rough grass of Bonchurch Down: "he with that springy, dancing step which he never entirely lost; while I, a much younger and very unsteady-footed child, stumbled along after them [Swinburne and his sister] among the younger fry, with frequent falls, and a feeling of pursuing the unattainable" (*PR*, 6). It was this cousin who would write to her often, corresponding about music, painting, and literature. He wrote about his admiration for Tennyson's poems, about the intricate complexities of a metre known as galliambics (found, as Swinburne mentions, in Tennyson's "Boadicea"), and about the relative ease of reading Euripides in

Greek: the two *Iphigenias* of Euripides, he informs her, "are generally very easy, and if you find the choruses hard you can skip or reserve them quite well" (*Letters*, I, 110). In addition to seeking her critical counsel—"I think you will agree with W.[atts Dunton] that my alterations [of *Rosamond, Queen of the Lombards*] are both poetic and moral improvements on the real story" (*Letters*, VI, 141),—he also advised her on her writing, providing her late in his life with a charming and detailed critique of *The Caveman*, a translation she had done of a modern Icelandic play.

Mary Gordon cited his dedication of *Rosamond* to her—"Scarce less in love than brother and sister born,/ Even all save brother and sister sealed at birth"—as evidence of the affection they held for one another. She also used it to suggest the ill-founded nature of a rumor concerning a romantic attachment between them. And although the logic of her argument—namely, that such a relationship would have been "an insult to our brother-and-sister footing" (*PR*, 5)—is less than satisfactory, her denial is almost certainly true.[4] Although Cecil Y. Lang has argued that Mary Gordon was indeed Swinburne's "lost love," the likelihood of any sexual relationship between them seems remote, not because they were cousins, but because, to use the nineteenth-century language of Edmund Gosse, "the generative instinct was very feebly developed in Swinburne." He enjoyed the company of women, but "never in any degree suggesting the amorous, or as though love

entered his mind" (*Letters*, VI, 243). What comes
forth from their relationship is not a romantic bond,
but a bond of mutual love and respect. They were two
people who seemed to have regarded each other with
affection and a sense of openness.

The fact that Swinburne kept one side of his life
completely apart from her, hoping that she would see
only his nobler or finer impulses, should not alter
our judgment of their relationship. There were at
least two worlds inhabited by Swinburne from the
early 1860s on—the world that Swinburne and Mary
Gordon shared, one of mutual background, music,
art, and literature—and the world reflected in letters
Swinburne wrote to men such as George Powell and
Richard Monckton Milnes (later Lord Houghton), a
world almost exclusively male, bawdy, often
obscene, with frequent references to the Marquis de
Sade, pornography, drunkenness, masochism, and
the literature of flagellation. It is characteristic of the
Victorian Age that these two worlds were kept apart
—or that at least the fiction of a total separation between them was maintained. Just as Mary Gordon
needed to retain an image of the favorite young
cousin she had known as a child, so too did Swinburne need someone who could say of him that "with
all his tremendous fund of wit or nonsense, nothing
profane, vulgar, or risqué ever cropped up" (*PR*,
32).

By the time Swinburne visited Mary Gordon and
her family at Northcourt during the fall and winter
of 1863-64, the world he kept apart from his cousin

was already too much with him. His favorite sister, Edith, had died in September 1863 after a long illness, and Swinburne himself was well on the way to becoming an alcoholic because of the strong but less than salutary influence of Richard Burton, the nineteenth-century adventurer, diplomat, and translator of *The 1001 Arabian Nights*.[5] Burton and Swinburne first met in 1861 and as Cecil Lang has suggested, their relationship seems to have been one of worshipped and worshipper: "it requires no imagination at all to understand how the virile bawdry and swagger of this cultured latter-day Elizabethan must have mesmerized the young Swinburne, sixteen years his junior" (*Letters*, I, 223n.). Burton was a giant of a man who could and did consume large amounts of liquor. And in spite of exaggerated notions of his own similar capabilities, Swinburne could keep pace with Burton's feats only with serious consequences to himself. By the time Swinburne visited his cousin late in 1863, he had already been admonished by Milnes, hardly a man of conservative morals or principles, for his excessive drinking.[6]

But this aspect of Swinburne's life does not seem to have intruded upon those months he spent at Northcourt. It was, as Mary Gordon would write, "the longest time he ever stayed with us continuously, and was a delightful as well as a memorable time" (*PR*, 20). The months he spent there represented more, however, than an opportunity to recuperate. It was also a time of intense creativity, for during this period Swinburne worked on *Atalanta in*

Calydon. "The first time," Mary Gordon writes, "I ever heard the opening chorus, 'When the hounds of spring are on Winter's traces', was on horseback and [I] know to this day the exact strip of road . . . where he repeated it to me" (*PR*, 20). She also recalls the setting within which the writing was done: "in our library, often alone with my mother and myself, much of the work was written out, and the table would be strewn with the big sheets of manuscript" (*PR*, 20-21). During this time, he was also trying to conclude his famous essay on William Blake. However, it was not a period devoted only to the high seriousness of Greek tragedy and the complexities of Blake's poetic myth. Both Mary Gordon and Swinburne loved moments that encouraged the comic and dramatic, and Swinburne's childlike enthusiasm and humor flourished in her company. She recounts how once, as a young boy, "he made us into a kind of tableau out of *Dombey and Son*—himself taking the part of Mrs. Skewton in her Bath chair. There was consultation as to who should be Carker—whoever could show the best set of teeth. I was eager to qualify for a part, and put on a tremendous grin, which I was told would do" (*PR*, 8-9). This same kind of creative playfulness extended into the Northcourt period—

> I think none of those who have since read and delighted in Atalanta would believe the amount of "nonsense" which was going on side by side with the famous work. We were both devoted to games of *bout rimes,* and used to set each other pages and pages of bouts, always of a comic nature. (*PR*, 21)

It was within this milieu of affection, creativity, and humor that the collaboration of *The Children of the Chapel* took place. And while it may have been seen initially by him as another literary exercise to clear his mind of the fatigue arising from his work on *Atalanta in Calydon* and Blake, it became much more than a diversion. Swinburne does not refer to the work in his letters, so we have only Mary Gordon's description of the collaborative process:

> at this time he wrote and gave to me, absolutely, for a boy's story which I was writing, a beautiful little "Morality" play, called The Pilgrimage of Pleasure. The book in which it appeared was called *The Children of the Chapel.* (*PR*, 21)

She adds to this general description some details that reveal an important side of Swinburne's talents:

> We had great amusement over the story, which I may almost call a joint production, he making suggestions and giving me endless references and information, the tale being historical. (*PR*, 22)

The usual image of Swinburne, that of an *enfant terrible* who shocked a staid and prudish Victorian society with his erotic and revolutionary poetry, is, of course, incomplete. The age was neither so staid nor so prudish as the image suggests, and Swinburne's talents extended far beyond his ability to rattle the bourgeoisie. He was also a fine scholar, an astute literary critic, and an enthusiastic student of history, especially of early English drama. He once, in fact, suggested to A. H. Bullen, the founder of the Shakespeare Head Press, that "every English play in existence down to 1640 must be worth reprinting on extrinsic if not on intrinsic grounds" (*Letters*, IV, 279-80). He wrote *Encyclopaedia Brittanica* articles on dramatists such as Beaumont and Fletcher, Marlowe, and Chapman—so many articles, as a matter of fact, that he once speculated that he was likely "to end as a minor English Diderot (the typical Encyclopaedist)" (*Letters*, IV, 205).

His greatest satisfaction, however, came when the *Encyclopaedia Brittanica* asked him to write an article on Mary Queen of Scots:

> Out of all the great historical "authorities" and "distinctions," all the specialists and scholars in the country, who might have been . . . asked to undertake it, . . . it is I, a mere poet, and therefore . . . a naturally feather-headed and untrustworthy sort of person, who am selected to undertake such a responsibility and assume such an authority as a biographer and historian. (*Letters*, IV, 263)

His "sheer self-satisfaction" shines through this letter, for he regarded the request as a high tribute to his "conscientiousness and carefulness" (*Letters*, IV, 263). His "industry and research, fairness and accuracy" (*Letters*, IV, 263), Swinburne's accurate if immodest appraisal of his previous historical research, are evident not only in the plays and articles he published, but in *The Children of the Chapel* as well. The amount of research and work that went into it, typical of the energy he devoted to projects that interested him, is suggested in Mary Gordon's Preface to the third edition of the novel:

The idea of the tale was suggested to me by finding Queen Elizabeth's commission to Thomas Gyles, in Dr. Burney's "History of Music." My cousin, Algernon Charles Swinburne, was staying at my father's house at the time, (1864); and from the first conception of my story he took the greatest interest in it, finding historical details for me, correcting anachronisms, suggesting or amending names, costumes, and incidents. In short, not a sentence was written without being read by him, not an episode worked out without his advice. Finally he proposed, since the "Children" were to act a play, that he should himself write a Morality for them. Hence the origin of "The Pilgrimage of Pleasure." My cousin gave it to me absolutely to be published without name and without acknowledgement.[7]

These creative energies that were seething in Swinburne during this period, unable to find sufficient release through his own writings, spilled over into her projects as well.[8] According to her own accounts, his presence is everywhere in the novel— from the historical details and costumes to the sentences he wrote and the episodes he helped to create. Since *The Children of the Chapel* was only Mary Gordon's second novel, she must have appreciated the assistance and advice of an older cousin who was already an accomplished poet and widely-read student of history and English literature. And on his part, the activity and pace of life during these months must have been salutary, occurring as they did at a place known to him since childhood and filled with memories and associations radically different from his London life. Swinburne's knowledge of the Elizabethan age was already extensive, and the chance to work on a novel that would enable him to draw upon and deepen this interest was one that he would not have turned down under any circumstances and certainly not when it meant an opportunity to work with Mary Gordon.

He stayed with the Gordons from October of 1863 through February of 1864; in March of that year, *The Children of the Chapel* was published. The novel went through three editions, the first two published by Joseph Masters and Son, and the third by Chatto and Windus. Joseph Masters published books on historical and musical subjects, such as *Maurice Favell; A Story of the Reform of Church Music in a Village; The Singers; or, A Story for Boys in a Country Church Choir*; and *Peter Noble the Royalist: A Historical Tale of the 17th Century*. Although the choice of Joseph Masters was thus a logical one, it must have struck an ironic chord within Swinburne, for Masters was also an active publisher of evangelical tracts and of children's stories laced with evangelical impulses. Several of his titles suggest the editorial bent of the firm: *Story of a Dream; A Mother's Version of the olden tale of "Little Red Riding Hood," wherein that tale is made to bear a Christian lesson: The Cottage in the Lane; or the Sad Effects of Indecision of Character; The Sprained Ancle; or, the Punishment of Forgetfulness;* and a lovely title, *I'm So Happy; or, the Reward of Sorrow Borne Religiously.*

While *The Children of the Chapel* was intended for young readers—Mary Gordon refers to it as "a boy's story"—it would most likely have been bought by parents; thus, like a number of titles published by Masters, it sought to combine enough intrigue and excitement to interest its young audience, with a moral or religious vein strong enough to make it acceptable to those with the purchasing power. In view of its intended audience, then, it is not at all surprising that Swinburne's name was excluded from the title page. He had not yet, of course, acquired that notoriety he would later come to possess, but his known association with men such as Richard Monckton Milnes and D. G. Rossetti—he had testified publicly at the inquest concerning the death of Elizabeth Siddal, Rossetti's wife, in 1862—would probably have been sufficient cause to prevent the publication of the novel; it would most certainly have been enough of a reason for a publishing firm such as Joseph Masters to reject it.

One of the primary features that make this novel distinct is, of course, Swinburne's role in creating it. And yet, both the setting and the initial concept for the plot reflect the expertise and interests of Mary Gordon. Because much of the novel is set within the Chapel Royal, it is directly concerned with music; and toward this art, Swinburne's attitude was primarily an intuitive one. Although one critic has referred to him as the "most unmusical of men" (*Letters*, I, xxx), Swinburne did, however, possess the capacity to enjoy music and the faculties to judge it. During his stay with the Gordon family, he wrote of how his "greatest pleasure just now is when M. [Mary Gordon] practices Handel on the organ; but I can hardly behave for delight at some of the choruses" (*Letters*, I, 93). And just as he would later make use of Wagner's music in his own creation of "Tristram of Lyonesse," so too did he assimilate, as only a poet could, the music of Handel:

> I care hardly more than I ever did for any minor music; but that [Handel] is an enjoyment which wants special language to describe it, being so unlike all others. It crams and crowds me with old and new verses, half-remembered and half-made, which new ones will hardly come straight afterwards; but under their influence I have done some more of my Atalanta which will be among my great doings if it keeps up with its own last scenes throughout.   (*Letters*, I, 93)

But while Swinburne later provided the wealth of historical details we find in the novel, it was Mary Gordon's reading of "Queen Elizabeth's commission to Thomas Gyle, in Dr. Burney's History of Music," that led to the original idea for *The Children of the Chapel*. Dr. Burney's book is Charles Burney's famous *A General History of Music, from the Earliest Ages to the Present Period* (1776-1789), and more specifically, his chapter on "Music in England during the XVI Century."[9]

In addition to discussing a number of the figures who later appear in *The Children of the Chapel*, such as William Byrd and Thomas Tallis, Burney also provides a history of the Chapel Royal, describing how children were supplied to choirs such as those of the Chapel Royal and St. Paul's:

> In the time of Henry VIII, when Music was more cultivated in England than it had ever been before, a similar power [of impressment] was given to the Deans of Cathedrals and collegiate churches for supplying their several choirs with children possessed of good voices by this arbitrary and oppressive method.[10]

The origin of the Chapel Royal itself is obscure, but by 1420, royal commissions were already authorizing the impressment of boys into it and other children's companies.[11] During the reigns of Henry VIII and Elizabeth I, in fact, the practice was so common that the various companies were actually stealing boys from one another. This unseemly behavior ultimately led to a royal decree first ordered by Henry VIII and used by subsequent monarchs exempting from such impressment boys serving in certain choirs. Queen Elizabeth's warrant, for example, reads: "we give power to the bearer of this to *take any singing men or boys* from any chapel, our own Household and St. Paul's only excepted."[12] It was such a commission that Thomas Gyles uses as authorization to impress the young Arthur Savile into the service of the Chapel Royal.

Many young boys, like Arthur, were taken away without any word being left for their parents. In fact, one of the major sources of information about this practice is the transcript of a complaint brought to the Star Chamber in 1601 by Henry Clifton of Norfolk. His son, thirteen-year-old Thomas, was seized on his way to school and taken to Blackfriar where, according to his father, he found him "amongste a companie of lewd and dissolute players."[13] The father immediately protested to the company's master, but was denied the return of his son; finally, however, after more than a year, his son was returned and the men responsible censured—not for abducting the boy, but for abducting him into a company of actors rather than singers. Although the boy companies were virtually to die out in England by the end of the sixteenth century, they were still quite strong in 1559, the year Arthur Savile was abducted, and the Chapel Royal was the most famous among them.[14] Its formal purpose was to provide music for the religious services of the Court; but in addition to this formal purpose, it was also extensively involved in dramatic performances.[15] Such was its dominance, as a matter of fact, that it was singled out in 1569 by a Puritan pamphlet entitled "The Children of the Chapel Stript and Whipt" for both its dramatic subjects and mannerisms:

> Even in her majesties chappel do these pretty upstart youths profane the Lordes day by the lascivious writhing of their tender limbs, and gorgeous decking of their apparel, in feigning bawdie fables gathered from idolatrous heathen poets.

"Plaies will never be supprest," continues the almost apoplectic writer, "while her majesties unfledged minions flaunt it in silkes and sattens. They had as well be at their Popish service, in the devil's garments."[16]

In emphasizing the choric and dramatic aspects of

the Chapel Royal, *The Children of the Chapel* accurately portrays the organization as it existed in the middle of the sixteenth century. A young Victorian reader would have learned, however, not only about the nature of Elizabethan drama and music, but also about the most famous musicians of the age. Richard Bower, Master of the Children of the Chapel from 1545-1561 and thus a servant of three different monarchs (Henry VIII, Edward VI, and Elizabeth I), is viewed as a hidden but omnipotent deity:

> [Arthur] had been living under a delusion, believing that in knowing him [Gyles] at least he knew the worst; whereas all this time there lurked above and behind a supreme, awful, though hidden power, of whom Gyles was but the agent. It would be difficult to describe the terror with which the poor boy was inspired by the idea of "old Master Bower." (133)

The young reader would have also become acquainted with Thomas Tallis and William Byrd, two of the most famous Elizabethan musicians and composers. William Byrd is one of the central figures of the novel and probably the closest thing in the work to a hero. Thomas Morley, who appears as a youth in the morality play in the part of Pleasure, was another well-known Elizabethan composer who, like Tallis and Byrd, enjoyed the exclusive rights to the printing of music.[17]

When the novel does stray from historical fact, it is often to accommodate the anticipated tastes of its nineteenth-century audience. There is, for example, no mention of the dominance of the Catholic religion within a group such as the Chapel Royal, nor is there any mention of the fact that William Byrd was throughout his life a Catholic at heart. In one incident in the novel, "one Master Woolmer, a Papist" (33) is "mobbed through the streets by a loyal public" for speaking disrespectfully of the Queen (33). And although the novel cannot condone such action, it does account for it:

> In the preceding reign, when the Romish religion was in the ascendant, great persecution had arisen, and much cruelty had been practised towards the Reformers. . . . Now . . . it was perhaps not wonderful that there should be so much bitterness of feelings towards the Romanists. (47-48)

The treatment of the "Papist" might not have been Christian, but it was certainly understandable. The novel also shares with the Puritan pamphlet a disapproval of some of the performances by the Children of the Chapel:

> I wish I could say that all the plays acted by the Children of the Chapels Royal were as innocent and instructive as "The Pilgrimage of Pleasure." The "Moralities" might be very well in their way, but I fear that many of the pieces which in those times were publicly performed by children were such as no child would nowadays be suffered to read. (179)

We hear in the same passages Mrs. Grundy's voice being raised not only against the corruption of youth and innocence, but also in praise of the superior moral climate of the nineteenth century:

we should be very thankful that our lot has been cast in happier times, when so much more thought and pains are given to teaching the young what is right and good, and keeping them from evil, than was the case in days gone by.

We also find evidence of a Victorian faith in spiritual and social evolution, a belief, to quote Tennyson, that "through the ages an increasing purpose runs / And the thoughts of men are widened with the process of the suns" ("Locksley Hall"). And although this faith was, as G. M. Trevelyan has suggested, "a very conditional affair"—Tennyson himself would later speak of "Evolution ever climbing after some ideal good,/ Reversion ever dragging Evolution in the mud"—there is little ambiguity evident in the above passage.[18] As I will later suggest, darker images of the Victorian Age do appear in the novel, rendering it more ambiguous, more troubling than the world described above. But such images do not appear on the surface of the novel.

The Children of the Chapel is constructed around a time-proved plot that has a universal appeal for readers, regardless of their age or the times in which they live. During a walk to school a youngster is kidnapped by a person of dubious character and taken to a strange and alien setting in which he must somehow survive by means of his wit and ingenuity. The novel ends happily, as one might expect, in that Arthur Savile is finally found by his parents who had long since given him up for dead. Instead of being taken home, however, he is left within the Chapel

Royal, his father being a "conscientious man, and loyal subject" who "regarded his son as a servant of the Queen" (177). After his voice breaks, Arthur is "placed at Eton by the Queen's appointment, to continue his education" (180).[19] Given Eton, however, as it existed in the sixteenth century, indeed well into the nineteenth century, such a reward would have been a mixed blessing for Arthur, who had already been brutalized in the Chapel Royal and could only expect more of the same at Eton. Since Swinburne himself had attended Eton, this particular twist of the plot might very well be a touch of bitter irony on his part.

In addition to containing enough adventure and intrigue to attract and retain a younger reading audience, *The Children of the Chapel* was also, like so many titles published during the age, intended to enlighten and improve. The lack of enthusiasm for devotional tracts and didactic fiction of our own age perhaps makes it difficult for us to understand the reading habits of the Victorian Age—although no more difficult probably than it would be for a Victorian to understand our devotion to books, equally didactic in their own ways, on the joys of jogging, sex, and self. Of the 45,000 books published in England between 1815 and 1851, over 10,000 were religious works, followed by history and geography (4900 titles). By way of comparison, there were approximately 3500 novels published.[20] And although fiction did, of course, gain in popularity as the century advanced, the novels being read were not necessarily those of the Brontës, Dickens, or George Eliot. One Manchester bookseller sold "an average of 6000 numbers *weekly* for each of a small library of creations like *Angelina, Elmira's Curse, Claude Deval, Ella the Outcast, Gentleman Jack, Gambler's Wife,* and so on, but only 250 *monthly* of Dickens and 200 of Bulwer-Lytton."[21] These numbers do not suggest that Dickens' novels did not sell—we know, on the contrary, that they did—but rather they suggest just how well the pulp novels sold.

While a large number of middle-class families would buy nothing but devotional literature, an even larger number sought to combine in their reading both amusement and moral improvement. Hannah More's stories, after all, sold hundreds of thousands of copies.[22] *The Children of the Chapel* is a descendant of such literature, albeit one whose evangelical flavor is more subtle perhaps than the religious literature of the earlier part of the century. The moral tenor of the novel is established quite early, for when we first meet Arthur Savile, he is "idly watching the proceedings of a fisherman" when he should be in school. The operative word here is *idly,* for we soon learn that "idleness was Arthur Savile's great fault; not lazy, but heedless idleness" (2). Idleness, especially when it infects a ten-year-old boy, becomes a pernicious failing, a moral and spiritual decay that will, unless checked, ultimately destroy. In places, *The Children of the Chapel* seems to subscribe to what one historian has characterized as the "principle formulated by Hannah More, namely, that the chief purpose of juvenile literature is to teach children that they are naturally depraved creatures."[23] It is this idleness that allows Arthur to be kidnapped by Master Gyles, and it is the same moral infection that brings about his first flogging: for although he was kidnapped and transported many miles on horseback with little food or sleep, his failure later that evening to memorize some dramatic lines is attributed to his habitual "listless idleness."

The ambiguous attitude of the age toward children—its impulse on one hand to idealize or sentimentalize them and, on the other, to view them as "naturally depraved," fit like Pip only to be "brought up by hand," is reflected in the ambivalence of the novel toward the subject of punishment. At one point, Arthur is beaten daily for a deed he did not commit, and in one moving passage we hear of the physical and psychic damage caused by such punishment:

> He seemed, even to himself, to be growing so strangely different from what he used to be; so dull and hardened and uncaring, as if all his senses were being beaten out of him. And indeed it could scarcely be otherwise when all his energies of mind and body were concentrated upon the one great daily effort of endurance. (58)

But after describing those "sickening hopes and doubts and fears that chased each other through his young brain" (58) and examining the consequences of such brutality, within a few pages the novel suggests rather different consequences. After William

Byrd intervenes and informs Gyles of the real culprits' identities, Arthur's beatings stop and we read
that:

> Arthur's spirits, relieved from the constant strain of
> endurance, regained their natural vivacity; and long
> before the outward scars of the rod were healed the
> memory of his weeks of trouble had been nearly
> obliterated from his childish mind.   (68-69)

The "childish mind" is seen here not only as a re-
pository for depraved thoughts and impressions that
must be controlled, but also as an organ of memory
whose retentive powers are blessedly limited, one
whose scars, in fact, heal much more quickly than
those of the skin. It is regarded in ways similar to
the eighteenth-century view of the mind of the insane
or simple, namely, as an organ that gave them protection from or even immunity to those cares and
anxieties that beset the rest of us.[24] But at the same
time that the childish mind was expected to heal
quickly, it also had to be responsive to suggestion,
education, and punishment; otherwise, the earnest-
ness and vigor of schoolmasters would be for naught.
Thus we read that not only was Arthur's mind healed
quickly from his sadistic treatment by Gyles, but also
that he was improved by it—an improvement, however, tainted by the evil influence of classmates whose
own natural depravity tends to diminish Gyles' good
works:

> Some of his [Arthur's] old failings had been driven
> out of him by Gyles' rod; but, on the other hand, his
> companions taught him and coerced him to do many

things which he had been brought up to think wrong,
and which led him into trouble either outward or
inward—frequently both. (70-71)

For those who do transgress or disobey, flogging is
not the only punishment to be expected. Borrowing
from evangelical tracts and literature, *The Children
of the Chapel* makes use of two frequent images of
retribution and punishment. When the boys decide
to secretly take a boat out on the Thames, we know
that a disaster will occur, and not just because Arthur
has had premonitory dreams. And sure enough, the
authors make use of a favorite evangelical motif in
which a Sunday boating expedition is run over by a
barge and all the sinners aboard killed. The boat is
capsized by a barge—in this case, the Queen's—and a
boy is drowned.[25] Arthur, too, almost drowns, an
experience that occasions beneficial self-scrutiny on
his part:

> so many naughty things that he had said and done
> came back to his recollection, things forgotten long
> ago; and in the last year, the many instances in which
> he had given way to his companions, in what at the
> time seemed but such trifling matters of conscience,
> and yet, looked at on the verge of that other life,
> were so great. . . . (84)

The other borrowed image is that of one being thrust
into a dark closet, there to contemplate the evil of
one's soul and the errors of one's ways.[26] When
Arthur allows a hawk he is training for the interlude
to escape, he is forced into such a dark closet. The
terror of such a situation is dwelt upon at length: "he

was sick and faint with hunger now, but what would it be by-and-by? He wondered if he should feel himself turning into a skeleton. . . ." (111). His fear, natural enough under the circumstances, of possible ghosts also contained within the walls causes him to press "his head against the ground with his eyes tightly closed, too frightened for tears" (113). Without inquiring into the potential consequences of such an experience, the novel suggests only that Arthur failed to remember those guardian spirits that watch over him and that his habits of the past year had caused him to lose "some of his simple faith and conscientiousness, some of his manly courage too" (113). Had he remained manly and remembered such spirits, "he would surely never have worked himself up into such an agony of fear" (113). Our immediate response is to suggest that it was probably the imagined presence of spirits, not their absence, that so terrified Arthur. In any case, he passes out from terror; he spends three more nights in the dark closet, his fitful sleep punctuated by "painful and confused dreams which troubled it" (113). As in the case of the floggings, there is no suggestion of the possible permanent effects of such an experience. On the contrary, he is released finally because he is needed at the rehearsal and they want him to be "bright and lively." Again, it is assumed that his "childish mind" recovers from all terror and horrors quickly and whatever scars may have been inflicted will heal quickly as well. Manly courage and religious faith, aided by a benevolently faulty memory are enough, it seems, to see a boy with proper pluck through almost any experience.

One dominant impulse within the novel, however, cannot be accounted for by either its evangelical traces or by the ambivalent attitudes of the age toward children. At one point, the novel asks its readers to compare their own fortunate state with that of those who lived in the sixteenth century and were "driven to their task by sharp words, blows, and floggings" (39). But as Swinburne could have informed his cousin, such blows and floggings continued well into the nineteenth century. There is, indeed, no reason to believe that Mary Gordon was not familiar with this aspect of English education—in her *Personal Recollections*, she remembers Swinburne describing "in an amusing manner how he and his companions were 'lodged and boarded in the schoolhouse', where he once overheard a flogging going on in the schoolroom, to which his Etonian ears were especially sensitive—and sympathetic" (*PR*, 25).

But while there is a great amount of flogging and physical brutality in the novel, it was nevertheless brought out by a publisher of children's literature and religious tracts; we can infer from this, I think, that it was not viewed by the age as being particularly violent or sadistic. Indeed, it is likely that schoolboys who read *The Children of the Chapel* would have been sympathetic to Arthur's plight, but would not have seen it as different from their own. For flogging, whatever the contempt and horror with which we regard it today, was not regarded by the nineteenth century as an aberration or as excessive cruelty, at least not by the schoolmasters and parents. As one historian has noted, "paradoxically, savagery which brutalized generally and terrified or enraged individually was not as a system unpopular."[27] In fact, Robert Southey was expelled from Westminster for having the temerity to suggest that "flogging was invented solely by the malice of the devil."[28] One of the most brutal of schoolmasters, Dr. John Keate, Headmaster of Eton for twenty-five years, was once laid up in bed for a week with strained muscles because he had flogged so many boys on the same day; and yet when he retired in 1834, the students gave him an affectionate farewell and over £600 worth of silver.[29]

The frequent presence of flagellation scenes in the novel cannot, however, be attributed strictly to a need for historical realism. Such scenes are too pervasive, unusually so, existing almost for their own sake and adding new implications to Mary Gordon's suggestion that in the Victorian period, "more thought and pains [were] given to teaching the young" (179). In such scenes, however, it is Swinburne's presence that we see. Shortly before her death, Mrs. Disney Leith told Lafourcade, Swinburne's biographer, of her cousin's creative role in the novel's flagellation scenes, a role not at all inconsistent with Swinburne's proclivities.[30] What is surprising is not that Swinburne would have written such scenes, but that he would have so revealed interests we may be certain were otherwise hidden from his cousin. Even more surprising is the fact that his cousin and their publisher would have agreed to the inclusion of so much brutality.

Swinburne was introduced to the writings of the Marquis de Sade by Richard Monckton Milnes in 1862, after having begged Milnes for more than a year to let him read them. In reading Sade, Swinburne found, in Lafourcade's words, "a mirror in which he spied the wildly distorted reflection of one side of his own nature" (*Lafourcade*, p. 105). It was not that Swinburne became introduced to sadism through Sade, for some of Swinburne's most sadistic passages occur in a comedy he wrote while still at Oxford.[31] Rather, what Sade did was to touch responsive chords already present; and the strength of Swinburne's response indicates how powerful those chords were. After 1862 Swinburne's letters are filled with allusions to Sade; and it seems that his collaborative effort with Mary Gordon on *The Children of the Chapel* provided him with yet another means of both acknowledging and releasing those impulses within him. And just as many of his most explicit letters are written in French, perhaps in homage to Sade himself, but more likely as a way of concealing and filtering the experiences described not only through language, but through a foreign language as well, so too did *The Children of the Chapel* require Swinburne to adapt and moderate his impulses to meet the demands of the novel as well as those of his audience. While such impulses are unmistakably present, they are filtered through the historical and fictive texture of the novel. Some of the scenes are undoubtedly drawn from Swinburne's own Eton days—in one of his letters, he speaks of living "under terror of flagellation by one's schoolmaster" (*Letters*, I, 67). Like Shelley before him, Swinburne had been treated brutally at Eton; and in such scenes, we find evidence of that institutionalized brutality that would lead Gladstone to suggest that it was "madness" to send a boy there who was not strong enough and caused Lord Chatham to observe that he "scarce observed a boy who was not cowed for life at Eton."[32]

Most of the scenes, however, probably represent the fruits of a rich fantasy life enclosing kernels of autobiographical fact. For even if we did not have Gosse's observation that Swinburne "experienced an ecstatic pleasure in letting his mind rest on flagellation" (*Letters*, VI, 244), the novel would suggest that such was the case. But because we are dealing here with the fantasy realm of psycho-drama, the categories of fact and fiction tend to keep merging into one another. For Swinburne knew such scenes not only from his Eton days, but also as an adult when he frequented a brothel in St. John's Wood presided over by "an elder lady, very respectable, who welcomed the guests and took the money" (*Letters*, VI, 245). Within, as Gosse describes it, "were two golden-haired and rouge-cheeked ladies [who] received, in luxuriously furnished rooms, gentlemen whom they consented to chastise for large sums" (*Letters*, VI, 245); and in a classic understatement,

Gosse observes that "Swinburne much impoverished himself in these games, which also must have been very bad for his health" (*Letters*, VI, 245). Freud, in fact, suggests that it is often the case that "the real-life performances" of masochists "tally completely with . . . [their] phantasies, whether the performances are carried out as an end in themselves or serve to induce potency and to lead to the sexual act."[33] In both cases, Freud continues, the content is the same—that "of being gagged, bound, painfully beaten, whipped, in some way maltreated, forced into unconditional obedience" (*CPW*, XIX, 162).

Given what Gosse refers to as the "feeble development" of Swinburne's "generative instinct" and what Swinburne's letters and later visits to "the grove of the Beloved Disciple" (*Letters*, I, 310) reveal about his sexual tendencies, it becomes quite evident, however incredible, that *The Children of the Chapel*, an eminently respectable Victorian novel, provided Swinburne with a release for his masturbatory fantasies, exciting him toward a potency otherwise not possible. The hero of the novel, Arthur Savile, possessing the same initials as Swinburne, is beaten, and in creating such a hero, Swinburne can observe, as spectator, himself being punished by an authority figure. And by projecting himself as a young boy, Swinburne also can satisfy one of the primary desires of the masochist—namely, that of being "treated like a small and helpless child, but, particularly, like a naughty child" (*CPW*, XIX, 162).

Although *The Children of the Chapel* cannot

qualify for inclusion within the underground flagellation literature of the period, it shares certain similarities in common with it. For example, in places the flogging scenes are almost formulaic, employing certain rituals of language and gesture that Steven Marcus has described in *The Other Victorians*:

> The accusation or admonition is delivered in ritual form, accompanied by dire threats. The antiphonal response is either defiance or supplication; if it is defiance, it soon gives way to supplication. These pleas for mercy go unheeded.[34]

In one fairly typical scene, Gyles plans to punish Arthur for falling asleep and failing to memorize his lessons: "it is plain that thou hast given no thought to the task during my absence, but I will teach thee to trifle with my commands" (28). Byrd tries to plead on Arthur's behalf—"Master, have pity," said Byrd undauntedly, "he is so young" (28). But in spite of Byrd's pleas, Arthur is beaten, receiving, we read, "the severest chastisement that had ever fallen to his lot. In vain he screamed and roared for mercy: there was none for him" (28). The difference between scenes such as this and those found in Victorian sado-masochistic literature is one of degree rather than of kind.

It is hard to know whether or not the audience of the novel would have been aware of the erotic or sexual overtones of such scenes. Since all of the scenes were included in the next two editions, however, we can probably infer that if parts of the novel offended certain readers, the offense was not strong enough or widespread enough to result in any editorial changes. In fact, we cannot even be sure whether Swinburne was aware of the implications of his sexual proclivities. It seems unlikely, however, that he could have been oblivious to the implications of his interests, even if his awareness was not fully conscious or self-confessed. Swinburne's letters do not reveal such an awareness, but they are almost always written to men who shared similar tastes and social class and often attended the same public school. An interest in flagellation seems to have been, like pony polo, a gentleman's pastime, and thus the tone of the letters is often that of an old-school tie relationship: such, for example, is the case in a letter to Lord Houghton about some reviews of *Atalanta in Calydon*:

> However, I'm not in much of a funk—a boy in my part of the school doesn't mind a swishing as much as a lower boy does. I can take a dozen cuts or so without wincing. Only let the Masters look out and not drive me to head a rebellion among the fellows of my own age, and bar them out of school. (*Letters*, I, 121)

At other times, it is difficult to determine where naiveté leaves off and reticence or deception begin. Gosse denies, for example, that Swinburne's flagellation literature was "bawdy": "it is the pain, and the excitement of the nerves caused by enduring pain, and seeing it inflicted, that are dwelt upon, and not any sexual phenomena" (*Letters*, VI, 247). Besides providing us with a strangely narrowed definition of "bawdy," Gosse seems to protest too much; Swinburne, in any case, certainly knew better.[35]

It is likely, as Steven Marcus has suggested, that the "literature of flagellation produced during the Victorian period . . . represents a kind of last-ditch compromise with and defense against homosexuality"; and it is in this respect that *The Children of the Chapel* acknowledges, obliquely through the screens of history and fiction, both the frequent cause and consequences of the brutality of the English public school system.[36] When we recall that more than twenty-five years later, Thomas Hardy would have to delete a scene in which Angel Clare carried Tess in his arms across a puddle of water, the inclusion of scenes such as we find in *The Children of the Chapel* become all the more astounding, attesting not only to the naiveté of Swinburne's collaborator and publisher, but to the sexual myopia—perhaps self-willed—of an age that would belie its own innocence when it reacted with such fury and outrage thirty-one years later at the trial of Oscar Wilde.

If some aspects of the novel remind us, as does Swinburne's life itself, of his demon-ridden soul and of those self-destructive impulses that inhabited one of the most creative and brilliant minds of the century, Swinburne's interlude, "The Pilgrimage of Pleasure," reminds us of those angels that also accompanied his voice, enabling him to make of the English language music such as had never been heard before. His "leaves of rhythm and rhyme" are in abundance in the play, and in its language we hear echoes of Swinburne's earlier poems. For by the early months of 1864 Swinburne had discovered those rhythms and images of his own poetic voice and had already written poems such as "Laus Veneris," "Faustine," "The Triumph of Time," and "Hymn to Proserpine." In making use of the inherited forms of early English drama, Swinburne found an opportunity to further explore these rhythms and sounds.

Echoes of his earlier poetry are heard throughout "The Pilgrimage of Pleasure," as, for example, in Death's admonition to Youth:

> Thou that wert full big shalt be shrunken to a span,
> Thou shalt be a loathly worm that wert a lordly man.
> Thou that madest thy bed of silk shalt have a bed of
>   mould,
> Thou whom furs have covered shalt be clad upon
>   with cold.   (158)

And in Life's realization of his ultimate fate:

> Lo, this is the last time that ever we twain shall meet,
> I am lean of my body and feeble of my feet;
> My goodly beauty is barren, fruit shall it never bear,
> But thorns and bitter ashes that are cast upon mine
>   hair.   (155)

But in spite of the death's-head we find within it, "The Pilgrimage of Pleasure" is for the most part an exercise in the comic mode, not Swinburne's usual medium, that justifies Lafourcade's suggestion that it "makes finer reading from a strictly poetical point of view than either The Queen Mother or Rosamond."[37]

Since Swinburne seems to have read virtually every

English play ever written, he was undoubtedly familiar with such famous interludes as John Heywood's *The Four P's*; and in "The Pilgrimage of Pleasure," he combines the allegorical devices of a morality play, including such figures as Life, Death, Vain Delight, Youth, and Discretion, with the specific characterization and earthiness we find in interludes. As well as being, however, an indefatigable student of English drama, Swinburne was also one of the great parodists in English literature, and in the interlude we hear certain parodic echoes of his own earlier poetry. For while we catch the reverberations of "Laus Veneris" and "Faustine" in lines such as "for Love of her sweet mouth he shall bide most bitter pain" (143) or "there is none happy man but he that sips and clips/ My goodly stately body and the love upon my lips" (149), we cannot take such eroticism seriously when it is continually juxtaposed to the comic lines of Gluttony:

> Ow, I am so full of flesh my skin goeth nigh to crack!
> I would not for a pound I bore my body on my back.
> . . . .
> A comfit with a caudle is a comfortable meat;
> A cony is the best beast of all that run on feet
> I love well butter'd ale, I would I had one drop;
> I pray thee, Mistress Sapience, hast thou never a sugar
>   sop?

Although much of the dialogue and action is comic in tone, the most sustained passage of the play, Death's final speech, is both forceful and serious, its cadences hauntingly beautiful and evocative. It is not only the *tour de force* of the interlude, but also one of the most compelling moments of the novel. It might also be among some of the finest poetry Swinburne wrote. While it is much too long to cite in full, a brief passage might perhaps give some indication of its power:

> Your mouths were hot with meat, your lips were sweet
> with wine,
> There was gold upon your feet, on your heads was
> gold most fine:
> For blasts of wind and rain ye shook not neither
> shrunk,
> Ye were clothèd with man's pain, with man's blood ye
> were drunk;
> Little heed ye had of tears and poor men's sighs,
> In your glory ye were glad, and ye glittered with your
> eyes.
> Ye said each man in his heart, "I shall live and see
> good days."
> Lo, as mire and clay thou art, even as mire on weary
> ways.
> Ye said each man, "I am fair, lo, my life in me stands
> fast."
> Turn ye, weep and rend your hair; what abideth at the
> last?
> For behold ye are all made bare, and your glory is over
> and past.   (164)

When we remember the life that Swinburne knew shortly before he wrote the morality play, and those tormented and pain-filled years that awaited him after he finished it, "The Pilgrimage of Pleasure," with its *memento mori* theme, reminding us of the transience and futility of the things and values of this world, must have come to possess a bittersweet significance for him.

Although Swinburne and Mary Gordon had once intended to publish "The Pilgrimage of Pleasure" separately under Swinburne's name, it is difficult to imagine it removed from the novel, its allegorical figures divorced from the fictional characters who perform them. The farcical action occurring offstage gives the play a life and energy that would be lost if the play were lifted from the novel. And in this respect, the relationship between "The Pilgrimage of Pleasure" and *The Children of the Chapel* seems emblematic of the novel itself. For its unique interest to students of cultural history and literature derives, in part, from the ways in which it contains the disparate impulses of the age itself. It is, like so many children's books, a novel for young readers that primarily reflects the values of the adult world and its attitudes toward the young. A historical novel that is scrupulously accurate and thorough in portraying an age removed from its own, it is also firmly rooted, in both its strengths and its weaknesses, in the nineteenth century. For in the evangelical impulses of the novel and the voice that arises from them, we find an attitude or set of perceptions that would not only cause some of the most eloquent artists of the age to plead for more gentleness and compassion toward the young—pleas, for example, such as we hear in *Oliver Twist*, *Jane Eyre*, and *Bleak House*—but would also help establish a climate in which that institutionalized brutality we see indirectly reflected in *The Children of the Chapel* would be condoned and legitimized. For if children are by nature depraved and corrupt, then that method which helps to chasten and subdue wayward spirits is to be encouraged.

The Children of the Chapel also contains evidence, however, of those darker, less public images of the age. The violence seen in certain aspects of the evangelical spirit of the age is shown in even greater relief by the more explicit violence we find in the borrowing of images and echoes from an underground literature. And, in turn, the juxtaposition of these two impulses can provide us with glimpses into those broader cultural implications of such violence. Like his genius, Swinburne's aberrations were individual, idiosyncratic, and particular; and yet they also reflect, however obliquely, the collective psyche of an age that condemned them with an enthusiasm matched only by the vigor with which it wrote about and practiced them. While no single work, however great, can ever embody all of the rich and ambiguous reflections of an age, each work of art, even lesser works, helps to illuminate certain images of the culture that produced it. And as such, *The Children of the Chapel* is truly an offspring of the nineteenth century, revealing, as it does, those various and particular expressions of piety and cruelty, of innocence and corruption that characterized the age itself. The novel also testifies, in its own fashion, to the capacity of art to hold contraries and different realities in a state of creative tension and to draw from this tension a toy of thought that would not only provide its creators with a happiness they would long remember, but would also provide us with evidence of how, as Coleridge and Keats so often remind us, art is born from within those mysterious, complex, and often perverse workings of the human imagination.

[1] Mary Gordon's first novel was *Mark Dennis, or the Engine Driver: a tale of the railway* (1859).

[2] Mrs. Disney Leith, *Algernon Charles Swinburne: Personal Recollections by his Cousin* (New York: G. P. Putnam, 1917), p. 3. Hereafter cited as *PR*.

[3] *The Swinburne Letters*, ed. Cecil Y. Lang (New Haven: Yale University Press, 1959), I, xxxii. Hereafter cited as *Letters*.

[4] See Cecil Y. Lang's article, "Swinburne's Lost Love," in *PMLA*, 74 (1959), 123-130. Lang suggests that Swinburne's love was not only lost and unrequited, but also that it might have been a love that Swinburne never disclosed to Mary Gordon.

[5] Edmund Gosse speaks of Swinburne's "marvellous gift for self-deception. Nothing was so easy as to 'get him off his legs' but he never appeared to be aware of it himself" (*Letters*, VI, 238).

[6] In a letter to Milnes, Swinburne refers to such admonishments: "It is very jolly here this time of year, but I might have preferred that forgotten sherry of yours to the hearing of declamations and expositions against it" (*Letters*, I, 67).

[7] *A Swinburne Library. A Catalog of Printed Books, Manuscripts and Autograph Letters*, collected by Thomas James Wise (London: Printed for Private Circulation Only, 1925), p. 16.

[8] During this collaboration, he was also aiding her with another novel she was writing, later to be published as *Trusty in Flight* (see *PR*, p. 22).

[9] Charles Burney, *A General History of Music, from the Earliest Ages to the Present Period*, ed. Frank Mercer (New York: Dover, 1957).

[10] Burney, *A General History of Music*, II, 29.

[11] *The Cambridge History of English Literature* suggests that its origin is "lost in antiquity, the date of its histrionic efforts is uncertain and the records of its later activity are woefully incomplete" (Cambridge: Cambridge U.P., 1908), VI, 314. E. K. Chambers is less ambiguous, tracing it back as far as the twelfth century (1135) and describing it as "an ancient part of the establishment of the Household," in *The Elizabethan Stage* (Oxford: Clarendon U.P., 1923), II, 24.

[12] Cited by Burney, II, 30.

[13] *The Elizabethan Stage*, II, 44.

[14] By the end of the sixteenth century, the children's companies had almost disappeared, probably because of economics rather than reform. One historian has suggested a possible reason for this phenomenon: "the choirs at the beginning of Elizabeth's reign trained much of the most competent bodies of actors, carefully dispersed as trained actors to men's companies or mixed companies, which of course became much more efficient than any company consisting of children only could be, and the children's companies had to give way!" G. E. P. Arkwright, "Elizabethan Choirboys and their Music," *Proceedings of the Musical Association*, 40th session (1913-1914), 136.

[15] See Walter L. Woodfill's *Musicians in English Society from Elizabeth to Charles I* (Princeton: Princeton U.P., 1953), p. 173. E. K. Chambers suggests, as a matter of fact, that "during the early years of Elizabeth's reign the drama is under the domination of the boy companies," in *The Elizabethan Stage*, II, 4. And of the Chapel Royal, J. H. Manley points out that "no other company . . . presents greater claims to having exercised a real leadership in the drama." See *Cambridge History of English Literature*, VI, 324.

[16] Quoted by Chambers, II, 34-35.

[17] See *Woodfill*, p. 169.

[18] *Ideas and Beliefs of the Victorians* (New York: E. P. Dutton, 1966), p. 51.

[19] Here, too, the novel is accurate. Cf. *Woodfill*: "As a rule, a boy who became a chorister in the Chapel Royal could expect to get an education, and had fair assurance of some kind of honorable career, probably in the Church" (p. 173).

[20] See R. K. Webb's "The Victorian Reading Public" in *From Dickens to Hardy*, ed. Boris Ford (London: Penguin, 1958), p. 206. In his *The English Common Reader* (Chicago: University of Chicago Press, 1963), Richard Altick points out that "the middle class, where evangelicalism was most at home, formed an insatiable market for the edifying tales and the serious didactic and inspirational works that flowed from pious pens" (p. 108).

[21] "The Victorian Reading Public," p. 217. Also see *The English Common Reader*, p. 123.

[22] F. K. Brown in his *The Fathers of the Victorians* (Cambridge: Cambridge U.P., 1961) quotes a contemporary of Hannah More's who, in writing of the incredible sales of her tracts, exclaims that "no such sales has ever been heard of in the annals of England," suggesting that "they had sold over two million by the end of the year (1795)" (p. 135). In his *The Victorian Debate: English Literature and Society 1832-1901* (New York: Basic Books, 1968), Raymond Chapman notes that "1,326,000 copies of tracts [were] issued by the Methodist Book Room in 1841 (p. 62).

[23] Maurice J. Quinlan, *Victorian Prelude: A History of English Manners, 1700-1830* (New York: Columbia U.P., 1941), p. 198.

[24] See Michel Foucault's *Madness and Civilization: A History of Insanity in the Age of Reason*, trans. Richard Howard (New York: Vintage, 1973), pp. 74-75. "It was common knowledge until the end of the eighteenth century that the insane could support the miseries of existence indefinitely" (p. 74).

[25] For more discussion of this motif, see *The Fathers of the Victorians*, p. 465.

[26] See Quinlan's discussion of Mrs. Sherwood's *The History of the Fairchild Family* (1818) for an example of this motif, in *The Victorian Prelude*, p. 198. Charles Lamb in his "Christ's Hospital Five-and-Thirty Years Ago" tells of a similar experience.

[27] Jonathan Gathorne-Hardy, *The Old School Tie: the Phenomenon of the English Public School* (New York: Viking, 1977), p. 43.

[28] Gathorne-Hardy, p. 42.

[29] Christopher Hollis, *Eton: A History* (London: Hollis and Carter, 1960), p. 220.

[30] Georges Lafourcade, *Swinburne: A Literary Biography* (London: G. Bell, 1932), p. 116.

[31] See LaFourcade, p. 105. The comedy was *Laugh and Lie Down*, written in 1858-59.

[32] Gathorne-Hardy, p. 66.

[33] "The Economic Problems of Masochism," in *The Complete Psychological Works of Sigmund Freud*, ed. James Strachey (London: Hogarth Press, 1955), XIX, 161-62. Hereafter cited as *CPW*

[34] Steven Marcus, *The Other Victorians: A Study of Sexuality and Pornography in Mid-Nineteenth-Century England* (New York: Basic Books, 1964), pp. 255-56.

[35] Cf. the sexual innuendoes of a letter he wrote to Lord Houghton:

I have read—in Southey's Miscellanies—a medieval legend to this effect: that a schoolboy flying from punishment took sanctuary in church and clung to a figure of the Blessed Virgin. Even thither, his breeches being down, his master followed, birch in hand; but in recompense of the child's faith, the master's lifted arm was stricken with paralysis, and only released at the boy's intervention. Were I in *that* boy's place, I should fly and cling to a living and fleshly statue of the Venus Callipyge (doubly appropriate)—which I think as competent *without a miracle* to stiffen any man's—arm. (*Letters*, I, 283)

[36] *The Other Victorians*, p. 260.

[37] Lafourcade, p. 116.

THE

CHILDREN OF THE CHAPEL

CHAPTER I

THE RIDE

It was a fine spring morning in the year 1559. The air was clear and mild, and the rays of the sun, though he had yet some hours to travel before reaching his midday height, were already gaining power ; nor did they shine less brightly three hundred years ago than now, upon the tall budding trees, the green meadows, and the calm river at the outskirts of the old country town of Ferryton.

Beside a gate opening upon one of those meadows was standing a young boy, whose dress and air, though not showy, betokened him to be the child of parents well off in the world. His little cap, with its drooping feather, shaded a handsome ruddy face, the complexion somewhat tanned by country air and sunshine, with small, straight features, lustrous hazel eyes, and soft

B

brown hair. His satchel hung carelessly from his arm as he stood leaning against the rail, idly watching the proceedings of a fisherman who was angling in the river at a little distance. I say idly, for the fact was, he ought to have been on his way to school then, and he had been standing there for at least ten minutes loitering. Idleness was Arthur Savile's great fault ; not lazy, but heedless idleness ; an idleness which made any kind of application, anything like work that did not fall in with his present fancy, distasteful to him. His father often spoke gravely to him about it, telling him that he was old enough now to correct himself of the fault, for he was ten years old ; old enough to go about his tasks because it was his duty to do so, even if he did not like it at the moment. He had scolded him and punished him too, and Arthur had taken both scolding and punishment in very good part, but had never yet thought seriously of setting himself to watch against his besetting failing.

So now he stood there, though he knew quite well that he should be late for school, wishing that he were the angler who was amusing himself, with no lessons to learn ; and thinking in his own mind how hard it was that he should be

obliged to spend the whole of that bright spring
morning shut up with his books. Not but
that if anyone had set Arthur to fish for an
hour he would not have grown heartily tired
of the occupation long before the time was up ;
but just then he would, or fancied he would,
have liked anything better than what happened
to be his present duty. It did not signify that
the pursuit he was watching was not particularly enlivening; at least he was putting off
the evil moment of beginning his distasteful
tasks.

His patience and that of the angler were
rewarded at last. There was a bite ; and Arthur
had the satisfaction of seeing the man land his
shining slippery victim. After which he be-
thought himself that it was really time to be
proceeding on his way, if he wished to avoid
public disgrace at school; so he swung his
satchel over his shoulder, pushed his cap
straight on his head, and set off at a brisk
pace, singing as he went the burden of an
old hunting carol.

He had not gone far before he heard the sound
of a horse's feet behind him. He turned, and
saw a horseman approaching, but continued his
way again unheeding, while the steady amble of

the horse kept pace for a while with his own hasty steps.

At length the rider checked his steed a little, at the same time exclaiming, " A good morning to you, young sir ; whither away so fast ? "

Arthur looked up at the speaker. He was a man of about thirty, spare and strongly made, with dark hair, a fresh complexion, keen grey eyes, and a face of which the naturally sharp expression was heightened by the short pointed beard. Something there might be a little severe in the eyes and mouth, but both were smiling now, and Arthur, as he gazed up at him, thought he looked very good-natured. From his dress Arthur took him for a gentleman of some rank : his horse, a sturdy animal, appeared fresh and cool, as if having but lately left its stable.

" I 'm going to school," was Arthur's frank answer to the stranger's question.

" To school are you, my lad ? and where ? "

" In Ferryton, sir."

" And what is your name ? "

" Arthur Savile."

" You were singing when I overtook you," continued the horseman, who seemed disposed to prolong the conversation, " what was your song ? "

" Oh, just an old carol."

" Suppose you sing it to me ; I have much liking for an old song, and it will enliven my journey."

" Sir, excuse me," said Arthur, " but I may not linger. I shall be late for school now."

" 'Tisn't far to your school, is it ? "

" A few paces down Ferryton High Street."

" Then we 'll make a bargain," said the stranger, pulling up his horse; "if you will sing me one verse of your song, I will give you a lift behind me into Ferryton. What say you ? "

Arthur's face brightened. He was as fond of fun as any boy in that century or this, and the temptation of a ride was a great one. It would make up his lost time too, and was very easily obtained ; for Arthur was not a shy boy, he was very fond of singing, and the strange gentleman looked so merry and kind. Arthur had a feeling somehow in his heart, however, that this was not doing quite as he should ; but he did not listen to it : as his manner was, he only thought of present gratification. So without considering whether his father would like him to be talking and riding with a complete stranger, he stopped, hesitated for a moment, and then began in a sweet clear silvery treble, the following carol:

" As I came by a green forest side
    I met with a forester that bade me abide,
    With hey go bet, hey go bet, hey go how,
    We shall have sport and game enow.

" Underneath a tree I did me set,
    And with a great hart anon I met !
    I bade let slip, and said hey go bet,
    With hey go bet, hey go bet how,
    We shall have sport and game enow."

Here Arthur paused for a moment, and glancing
up, caught the eye of his listener fixed upon him
in grave attention : his features had assumed
their natural expression, and it was one of such
sternness that the boy felt almost afraid.

" Go on, pray," said the stranger, seeing him
hesitate, " there is surely another verse.   It is
very well sung."

Arthur's vanity was flattered, and he proceeded,

" I had not stand there but a while,
    Not the mountenaunce of a mile,
    There came a great hart without guile ;
    There he goeth, there he goeth,
    With hey go bet, hey go bet how,
    We shall have sport and game enow.

" Talbot, my hound, with a merry taste,
All about the green-wood he gan cast ;
I took my horn and blew him a blast,
With tro, ro, ro, ro : tro, ro, ro, ro ;
With hey go bet, hey go bet how,
We shall have sport and game enow.
There he goeth, there he goeth,
With hey go bet, hey go bet how,
We shall have sport and game enow."

Arthur had gained more confidence as he
went on, and in the latter verse did justice to
his voice, which was really beautiful—true
and clear and high, like the notes of a bird.
Apparently it was not lost upon his listener, for
he smiled to himself a smile of great satisfaction,
exclaiming as Arthur stopped, " Bravely sung !
I have seldom heard an untaught voice so good."

" Oh, but we sing at home," said Arthur,
feeling a little injured at the qualification. " We
sing glees and carols—and the plain-song in the
Church."

" You do ? That is well. And now, young
sir, mount, if you will ride, for I have a journey
before me, and I may not waste my time." He
drew his horse up beside the bank as he spoke :
Arthur climbing it, sprang nimbly therefrom
upon the animal's broad glossy back, behind

his new friend, who bade him sit firmly, and keep a tight hold, and then put his horse into a quick trot.

It was great fun, certainly. Nobody that could have seen Arthur's merry rosy cheeks and laughing eyes, as he bumped up and down upon the great trotting horse, with his curly hair and his long feather shaking in the wind, would have doubted his enjoyment of his ride. But the pace was very rough, and he was not accustomed to the motion of a large horse, so it was as much as he could do, by clinging fast to his companion, to keep his seat at all. Just as they were crossing the bridge which spanned the river at the entrance to the town, a gust of wind snatched his cap from his head, and bore it away into the water. He turned to look after it—it was gone, and there was no help for it ; and almost before he had time to think whither he was going, the horse had passed through the whole length of High Street, leaving the Grammar School far behind.

Arthur wondered when his friend was going to stop—whether the horse were running away, half wishing to get off, yet sorry that his ride must soon come to an end. Not so soon as he fancied, however, for it was not until they had passed quite out of the town, that the stranger slackened his pace somewhat, and the decreased motion gave Arthur breath and opportunity to say, " Please, sir, we have passed the school a long way."

" Have we ? you should have told me before."

" And I shall be very late," continued the boy, rather timidly.

" Can't help it now," was the short answer. " I have not time to go back. Suppose, as we have left the town behind us thus far, you journey on with me, and visit my boys."

" Is it far to go ? " inquired Arthur.

" Not so very far."

" Will you take me home to-night ? "

" Surely."

There was another temptation for Arthur. A holiday, a double ride, a visit to companions of his own age ! There was no drawing back. And perhaps drawing back on his part would have availed little just then, for as they reached some smooth level ground, the stranger pressed his horse's side, and the former rough rapid pace was resumed.

" Your name is Arthur Savile, you said," was his observation, the next time that he drew rein; " whose boy are you ? "

"I'm the eldest son of Master John Savile, of Ferry Grange," answered Arthur.

"You have brothers?"

"One little brother, and two sisters."

"How old are you?"

"Ten last birthday."

"You are strong and hearty?"

"Yes," replied Arthur, a little surprised at so much questioning. "How many little boys have you, sir?" he ventured to ask, for he was curious to hear about his future friends.

"How many? there are somewhat about a dozen of them."

"How old are they?"

"They are of different ages, of course," and with that he put the horse into a trot again.

"I'm tired of trotting," said Arthur at last, rather unceremoniously, "it's so shaky; are we far off from where you live?"

"I answered that question a short while since," was the reply of the stranger, in a tone that seemed to Arthur a little harsh.

"But we have ridden a long stretch since that."

"A long stretch, quotha! Did you never ride half a mile from your father's doors, boy, that you call this a long stretch?"

"Oh, yes! but not on such a large horse."

They were ascending a hill, and the man presently told Arthur, who was clinging to him with both hands, not to hang to him like a log.

"I can't keep on without holding," objected Arthur, "the horse's back is so slippery."

"Stay!" cried the other, pulling up, "if you are fearful of falling, I will make you secure." He drew from under his cloak a long leathern strap, and bidding Arthur pass it around his waist, buckled it in front of his own. Arthur was thus free to unclasp his aching arms without fear of falling, which was a relief. He was beginning to get very tired of the jolting trot, however, and was really thankful when the stranger pulled up his hot horse at the door of a wayside inn.

"Is this where you live?" he asked, as the unknown rider unbuckled the strap and dismounted.

"Peace with thy simple questions!" was the answer. "Truly, I did not know that I bore the appearance of a country innkeeper!" Arthur wondered how he could have been indeed so simple as to ask, and was afraid he had offended his companion, as the latter walked into the house without further noticing him.

Entering the parlour, he sat down in one of the high oaken chairs, flinging aside cap and cloak, after desiring to have some refreshment brought at once. Arthur followed him, seating himself opposite ; the ride had made him hungry, and he looked up rather eagerly, as the good woman of the house brought in a plentiful supply of meat, bread, and beer, which she set before them on the table. He was on the point of helping himself, when his companion suddenly exclaimed, " Where are your manners, boy ? Get up and wait."

" I am not your serving-man ! " said Arthur, firing up at the way of speaking.

" Serving-man or not, who travels with me obeys my commands. Bring me the bread, knave."

Arthur obeyed, though not with a very good grace, and as he did so, dropped a piece of bread upon the floor. The man dealt him a cuff. Arthur's face reddened, and he turned round, surprised and angry.

" Poor child," said the landlady, whose interest had been awakened by the bright-looking handsome boy. " He is, maybe, unused to wait at table."

" I am not—I am not his serving-man ! "

repeated Arthur, when he had found his tongue.
" I 'm Arthur Savile of Ferry Grange, and he has
no right to command me. I 'm only going with
him because it is my pleasure, and I won't go
any further."

" Ha ! say you so ? " said the stranger, with
a cool smile that irritated the boy further.
" You should have thought of that before you
were so ready to take a lift on my horse. You
must follow my fortunes now, and be content."

" But you have dealt falsely with me ! "
exclaimed Arthur, and encouraged by the
sympathy expressed in the countenances of the
hostess and her daughter, who were standing by,
he went on ; " You said first you would take me
to school, and you passed it by ; you promised
you would take me to see your little boys, and
you 've brought me to this place, and treat me
like a menial knave. I won't go a step further
with you."

" Very well, sir : you will arrive at Ferryton
doubtless by to-morrow morn."

Arthur looked blank, as he remembered the
dangers and difficulties of a solitary journey—
for travelling then was not what it now is—
then turning to the woman he said, " You will
direct me, you will help me, will you not ? "

" Surely, young sir," was her answer ; " we have a strong horse, and my husband will convey you safely to Ferryton."

" Thanks, good woman," said Arthur, " my father will pay him well."

" He will gladly do it unpaid for your sweet young face, sir," said she with a smile as Arthur looked up at her with such frank, eager gratitude ; but the stranger broke in with, " You may spare your breath, mistress, and your honeyed words. The boy is of my following, and goes with me."

" That is false," burst out indignant Arthur, and the hostess rejoined, " The boy's story has truth on the face of it. Who art thou, to deal with the Queen's free lieges after this sort ? "

" Meddle not where thou hast no concern," was the answer.

" It concerns any honest person when they see a child in distress," answered the woman undauntedly, " and it seems to me that thou canst have no right to detain him against his will, if what he says be true."

" You are wonderfully free of speech, woman, to one who acts in the Queen's name, and with the Queen's authority."

" How can that be ? " asked Arthur in a

mixture of surprise and terror, " I never saw you
before ; I don't even know who you are."

" Her Majesty the Queen," interposed the
landlady, " is surely too kind and gracious a
lady to permit aught so unjust——"

" I care not to prolong this scene," said the
stranger coolly. " If my word is not enough,
perhaps the sight of Her Majesty's Commission
may convince your simple minds." Arthur
for once in his life heartily wished himself safely
within the walls of Ferryton Grammar School, and
a hundred terrible fears darted into his mind,
as the man drew forth from his pocket an official-
looking document bearing the Royal Signature,
and laid it angrily down upon the table.

Reading was not among the accomplishments
of the good woman of the inn, but turning pale
at the sight of the mysterious paper, she appealed
to her husband to decipher its contents. Arthur
however was a quick scholar, and pressing close
to the landlord's side he scanned the sheet, his
eyes dilating with horror as he did so. It ran
as follows :—

" ELIZABETH R.

" WHEREAS we have authorised our
servaunte, Thomas Gyles, to take up such apte

and meete children as are most fitt to be instructed and framed in the arte and science of Musicke and singing as may be had and founde out within any place of this our realme of England or Wales, to be by his education and bringing up made meete and hable to serve us in that behalf when our pleasure is to call for them. WEE therefore by the tenoure of these presents will and require you that ye permitt and suffer from henceforthe our said servaunte Thomas Gyles . . . to take up . . . suche childe and children as he . . . shall find and like of, and the same childe and children, by virtue hereof, for the use and service aforesaid . . . . to bring awaye without anye your lette, contradictions, staye, or interruptions to the contrarie. CHARGINGE and commanding you, and everie of you, to be aydinge, helpinge, and assistinge to the above named Thomas Gyles . . . in and aboute the execution of the premisses for the more spedie, effectuall, and better accomplyshing thereof from tyme to tyme, as you and everie of you doe tender our will and pleasure, and will answere for doinge the contrarie at your perille."

" Does it mean me ? does it mean you ? "

said Arthur, looking from one to the other in fear and bewilderment.

"Does it appear otherwise to thee?" said the stranger, enjoying the poor child's confusion; "is it so menial an office to be Her Majesty's singing boy, that thou shouldst pull so dismal a face?"

"But to leave home, my mother, my father—and they do not know! Oh, how I wish I had never sung that song!" and he could no longer keep back the struggling tears.

There was no pity in the face of Thomas Gyles. He pushed aside his trencher, rose from his chair, took up his hat, and said, laying no very gentle hand on Arthur's shoulder, "Waste no more time in vain wishes, if you will eat. This is the last stage, and I must ride hard if I would reach London ere nightfall." After which he stalked out of the room to see if his horse were sufficiently rested.

Poor Arthur sobbed and cried bitterly, clinging to the hostess, and refused her offers of food, only entreating to be sent home, to be taken away from that cruel man. The kind-hearted woman could hardly keep from tears herself, and looked round as though she would willingly have hidden him in the first cupboard, but that

c

terrible " at your perille " was not to be trifled
with in those days. She only fondled and kissed
the unhappy child, coaxing him to eat with the
most tempting morsels which remained on the
board, and at length he yielded so far as to take
a piece of bread and meat. He had not finished
his meal when his captor re-entered.

" I am ready to proceed," he said, flinging
his reckoning down before the landlady. " Come,
boy, bestir thyself." Arthur bolted his last
mouthful, but sat still, putting on an expression
of obstinacy. Gyles lifted him up by the collar
as if he had been a puppy or a kitten, carried him
out of the house, and after mounting his tall
horse, received him from the hands of the landlord,
and secured him by the strap to his own person
as before, as coolly as if Arthur were a mere
bundle of luggage. This done, he put spurs to
his horse, and rode off at a sharp pace.

Poor Arthur understood it all now: why
he had been coaxed to sing, and tempted to ride ;
why he had been carried so fast through the
town, and why Master Gyles was so careful to
fasten him to keep him from falling. He was
a prisoner, and nobody could help him, no one
rescue him. It would take too long to tell of
all the dreadful, vague fears that came into his

mind as he jolted along behind Master Gyles :
he would not have dared to ask any more questions even had he had the spirits for talking,
so he sat in silent misery, indulging his gloomy
thoughts, till he was almost too tired with the
rough, unceasing motion to think or care what
became of him. He scarcely looked up even
when they reached London, though he had
never seen the great city before, and had often
wished to go there. It was growing late in the
evening : the twilight was deepening, and the
narrow streets,—which were very different in
those days from what they are at present—looked
dark and gloomy. The tired horse stumbled
as, with drooping head, it stepped among the
rough stones which beset its path. Arthur thought
the houses and streets would never end, but at
length his captor drew bridle before the door of
one of those high dismal-looking buildings.

Here he dismounted, and entered the house,
bidding the boy follow him. Arthur was too tired
and stupefied to resist : he groped mechanically
behind the tall figure of Thomas Gyles along a
dark narrow passage, at the end of which he
found himself in a low long hall, with benches
in the midst, and a table on which a rushlight
was dimly burning. By its light Arthur perceived

a little knot of boys gathered together at one end of the room : a youth apparently about fifteen or sixteen was seated alone at the table writing.

" These be thy fellows, boy," said Master Gyles, turning to Arthur and pointing to the group ; after which he seated himself in a high oaken chair at the opposite end of the hall, leaving Arthur to improve his acquaintance with his new companions as best he might. They instantly surrounded him, and a shower of questions, " What is your name ? " " whence come you ? " " what part do you sing ? " and the like, assailed him on all sides.

At the sight of some of his own kind, and the sound of their voices, Arthur brightened up a little, sufficiently to answer. The sharp eyes of the boys quickly perceived the traces of tears on the countenance of their new schoolfellow. " Has Master Gyles beaten you ? " was the next question.

" Yes—no—wherefore should he beat me ? " asked Arthur.

" Wherefore ? ask himself," said one boy in a tone not loud enough to be heard beyond their own group.

" Does he often beat you ? "

" Doesn't he ? you 'll soon find that out. Ten floggings a day is the least you may expect."

" Oh, I wish—I wish——" began poor Arthur, and paused.

" What do you wish ? "

" That I had never met him this morning. But tell me, what tasks do you have to do ? "

" Oh ! we sing the pryck-song, and act plays."

" Do you like it ? " asked Arthur.

" Like it ? wait till one day has passed over your head, and then ask yourself," cried a big boy with a loud laugh ; " like it, quotha ! "

" The plays are the best," said another, " I suppose you 'll have to act—can you ? "

" No ; I never did."

" Well, then, I wish you joy of learning. You 'll have to be a lady. We 're getting up a play now, but the parts are all cast."

" I won't be a lady," said Arthur, " I 'll be a man, and wear a sword."

" Oh, no, you 'll have to be a woman. All the little ones take women's parts."

" I 'm not a little one," objected Arthur indignantly, " I 'm the oldest of four at home. I 'm ten years old."

This announcement was received with another explosion of laughter, and sundry cries of " Ho, old

master Wisdom, where is thy staff ? " " Surely he
will take the bass part in the Chapel," and so forth.

" Arthur Savile," interposed the awful voice
of Thomas Gyles from the other end of the room,
" methinks thy time might be better employed
than in idle chatter with thy comrades. Come
hither, and learn this task, that I may judge
somewhat of thy parts and memory." He had
risen from his chair, and now approaching the
table placed before Arthur an open book, marking
a passage therein. " Let me hear it repeated
without fault by supper time."

It was a tolerably long soliloquy in a play.
Arthur's heart sank, as he looked at it, with a
dull hopeless feeling of despair. Learning by
heart was to him the most difficult practice at
the best of times ; and now at the end of the day,
when he was so tired and sleepy and miserable,
to be given this unlooked-for task was hard indeed.
He glanced up imploringly at his master ; but
Gyles had turned away, and presently afterwards
left the room.

Arthur read the lines over once ; they seemed
to have no meaning to his bewildered senses, and
as to committing them to memory, it was in vain
to attempt it. He sat, resting his elbows on the
table and his chin on his hands, the book lying

open before him, but his eyes fixed on vacancy.
Then he turned them upon the big boy, who was
still writing opposite to him : writing, as Arthur
now saw, music. The face of this youth though
not strictly handsome was pleasant in its expression, with a look of much intelligence in the clear,
grave eyes bending over his work, and the wide
forehead. He had not even looked up when
Arthur came to the table, so absorbed was he in
his writing, and Arthur began to wonder whether
he were a scholar like the rest, or another master.
If Arthur had copied his diligence a little more
and wondered a little less, it might have been
better for him ; as it was, he sat in the same
listless idleness till some of the younger boys
came round him, half teasing, half tempting
him to play. He did not long resist them, and
when Master Gyles returned, he found Arthur
romping with the group in the corner, the play
book lying open on the table.

" Is thy lesson learnt ? " he asked.

Arthur hung down his head. " No, sir," he
mumbled very low, " I couldn't."

" Couldn't ! " repeated Gyles wrathfully, and
a succession of heavy blows fell upon the luckless
boy's cheeks and ears ; " tell me that a second
time, boy, and thou shalt have cause to remember

it. Now go into yonder corner and learn thy task, and no supper shalt thou taste till it is finished." He then bade the other boys clear the long table for supper, which was quickly done, and the meal spread.

Poor Arthur stole away sobbing into a corner where scarcely any light fell upon his book, while the others sat down to supper. It seemed harder than ever to learn now; and to add to his misery the other boys turned round at him from time to time with a taunt or a jeer. One only, the older boy who had been writing at the table, seemed to be touched with some compassion for his fate. After looking at him for a time silently, he ventured to say to his master, " Sir, if the poor child go supperless, he will have no voice wherewith to chant to-morrow."

" That concerns thee not, William Byrd," said Gyles sternly; but after a while he seemed to see the force of the remark, as he suddenly called to Arthur and bade him take some meat.

Arthur was too hungry, after his long journey, to disregard the permission to eat, though he looked very crestfallen as he stole up to the table. He was refreshed however by what he took, but was much dismayed on finding that his task was not to be remitted that night. He was bidden resume it as soon as the table was again cleared.

"Still over thy exercise, Will ? " said Gyles, as the boy resumed his seat and his writing opposite to Arthur.

"Yes, sir," was the answer, "I promised Master Tallis that I would have it ready by to-morrow, if possible."

"See, then, that the idle young rogue there does not leave his lesson till it is perfected," said his master, and again left the room.

Arthur sat down to his task with something more like an attempt at application. But small success attended his efforts. He had been sleepy before, and now he could hardly keep his eyes open. It was past his usual bed-time, and he was, besides, tired out with the events of the day. Presently another boy came and peeped over his shoulder.

"Is the lesson learnt ? " he asked.

"Oh, no," sighed poor Arthur.

"Why, how much have you got to learn ? "

"All this," pointing to the piece.

"Only that ! why any one could knock that off in the twinkling of an eye."

"What will he do when he has to get up his part ? " suggested another boy.

"Come, come, lad, make haste and learn," said a third, thumping Arthur upon the back; "old Gyles will be here presently, and then, and then!" the sentence was concluded by a malicious grin.

"Shan't we see the big rod come out!"

"Ho, master, make ready," cried yet another tormentor, pretending to make a swish at Arthur with his doubled fist.

The poor child looked around him, scared. The small portion of his lesson that was beginning to take hold of his reluctant memory fled hopelessly before the spiteful merriment of his comrades. They, hardened by similar treatment before, only exulted in his distress, becoming every moment more overbearing.

"Peace with your noise!" at length exclaimed William Byrd, looking up; "how can one do anything if ye keep up such a tumult around him?"

"Mind thy musty old exercise!" shouted a chorus of voices in answer.

"I tell you what," said Byrd, rising, "if you do not keep your idle hands and tongues off the boy, I will make you."

"Try, try!" They crowded round Arthur directly; they seized him by both arms; they whisked his book away from before him ; they shouted all kinds of nonsense lines into his ears. Byrd scrambled across the table, and a regular battle began ; he dealing out thumps indiscriminately, they dodging, kicking, striking at him, but all the time keeping their hold on Arthur. In the scuffle the inkhorn on the table was upset, and the ink thrown over Byrd's writing.

" There, there, behold ! " cried the triumphant enemies, " Master Tallis won't have the exercise so soon as he reckoned."

" Gyles is coming," cried one of the group in a voice of sudden alarm, and a general rush to the end of the hall ensued. When Gyles re-entered he found only Byrd standing by the table.

" Arthur Savile, come and repeat thy lesson."

Arthur crept up to the table with drooping head, amidst the smothered laughing of his comrades. He dared not confess a second time that the lesson was unlearnt. He allowed his master to take up the book, with a sort of wild hope that by some lucky chance the lines might occur to his memory. But no such luck was his : he repeated the first line, and then stuck fast.

" You have not tried to learn this."

Arthur made no answer, but burst into tears.

" This passes sufferance," said the master,

with a quiet anger which to Arthur was very terrible, "it is plain that thou hast given no thought to the task during my absence, but I will teach thee to trifle with my commands. Bring me the rod, William Byrd."

"Sir," said Byrd courageously, "I doubt if the poor knave can learn to-night. He is so drowsy that he can scarce hold up his head, and the others have tempted him to play."

"He is an idle scoundrel," said Gyles, growing more indignant at the delay, "and thou art another for defending him. Bring me the rod, I say. Drowsy, quotha!" he continued, as Byrd no longer dared to disobey, but handed him his weapon, "I have that in hand that shall wake him up. Strip, sir," and he turned to the trembling Arthur, who now fully awakened, was crying bitterly.

"Master, have pity," said Byrd undauntedly, "he is so young."

"Thy turn shall come next, William Byrd," was all the answer he received, as Gyles turned to his first victim. Arthur was held by two bigger boys, and received the severest chastisement that had ever fallen to his lot. In vain he screamed and roared for mercy : there was none for him.

When at last he was released, Gyles turned to the senior boy. " Now, sir, art thou ready ? "

" Wherefore, master ? " said Byrd.

" Ask thyself, next time thou art tempted to meddle in another's concerns," said Gyles. Byrd shared Arthur's fate, but without a word or a tear.

" Now, boy, we will see if thou art sufficiently aroused to apply thyself. The rest may go to bed."

" May I stay, sir ? " asked Byrd, " I have to rewrite my exercise."

" Stay if thou wilt, I care not," was the rough permission, and Gyles marshalling the rest of his troop out of the hall, the companions in suffering were left alone at the table as before.

Very little of Byrd's exercise, however, was done that night. In a few moments he crossed over to where Arthur stood in blank despondency.

" Now, boy," he said, looking over Arthur's shoulder, " where is your difficulty ? "

" All, everything," was the mournful answer.

" Let us see if we can conquer it together," continued Byrd, hopefully ; " we will read it over twenty times. You begin."

Arthur stumbled over the lines in a most lamentable voice. Then Byrd read them, but in a different tone and manner—almost as if he were acting the part. The words began to have some sense to Arthur now, and he looked up almost brightly at his friend. Like a young horse that refuses to pull alone, but puts its shoulder to the collar readily when harnessed beside another, Arthur began to put forth a little of the power of his mind when he found himself helped. He repeated the lines after his companion ; and then Byrd explained to him their place in the plot of the play—by whom they were repeated. Arthur became quite interested, and in an incredibly short time was able to recite them as correctly, and nearly as emphatically, as Byrd himself. Byrd praised his success, and told him that he would make a good actor some day.

" You must repeat them so to Gyles to-morrow ; he will be pleased. We shall not see him again to-night ; we will go to bed now."

" But you have not finished your writing," said Arthur, whose misfortunes had given him a little thoughtfulness for others ; " are you not afraid of being beaten again ? "

" No," answered Byrd ; " Master Tallis never beats me."

" Who is Master Tallis ? " inquired Arthur. " Is he another master ? "

" Not yours—mine," replied Byrd with a smile. " He instructs me in the science of music."

" Is he over Master Gyles ? "

" No, he is one of the gentlemen of the Chapel, and plays the organs sometimes. He has nothing to do with Gyles, nor shall I have much longer ; I shall leave this summer."

" Oh, how glad you must be ! "

" You may say glad," answered Byrd ; " though it is not so bad for me as for some of them ; and I don't care about old Gyles as I used."

" How long shall I stay here ? " Arthur asked.

" That will be according to Gyles' and Her Majesty's will and pleasure. Till your voice breaks, most likely."

" Oh, dear ! I hope I shall soon break it ! " cried Arthur earnestly.

And so they departed to bed : Byrd carrying the light, Arthur following him closely, feeling a kind of shuddering vague terror as they passed through the dark passage.

The dormitory was over the hall—like it, low and long and dark; there were rows of pallets down the sides. All the other boys were in bed ; most of them were asleep, or pretending to be so, as the two belated ones entered.

" There is but this bed unoccupied," said Byrd,
after due observation with his rushlight. " We
two can share."

How glad poor Arthur was to lay his head on
the pillow, after the events of this unhappy day,
may be more easily imagined than described.   Yet
even then his trials were not all over.   As soon
as the light was out some of the supposed sleepers
roused up and showed a manifest disposition to
talk, if nothing worse.   Arthur's next neighbour,
one of those who had been most forward in
teasing him downstairs, enlivened his last waking
thoughts with minute descriptions of the torments
commonly practised by Master Gyles upon his
victims, rendered more forcible doubtless by
painful experience on the narrator's part.

And when at length he was tired, and Arthur
dropped asleep, it was little better.   The events
of the day came back to him in a confused,
painful jumble ; he was surrounded by that
tormenting crowd, trying to learn a task of infinite
length, and hopelessly unintelligible ; he was
trembling under the great rod, or else he was
bumping upon the tall rough horse, tightly
strapped to Master Gyles, with his square shoulders
and cloak always before him, jolting on over an
endless succession of country, down an endless

succession of dark narrow streets, till the horse made a tremendous stumble—and with a painful start the poor boy awoke to the consciousness of his trouble, his loneliness, and a strange uncomfortable sense of having forgotten something—he was not very long in recollecting what.

Arthur had been brought up by a good and thoughtful mother, whose love and care had been extended to the souls as well as the bodies of her children. From his early years she had taught him to repeat a short simple prayer, night and morning, and a verse of a hymn, before lying down to rest. And with all his heedlessness, he had hitherto not neglected the habit—perhaps he had had no temptation to do so, living in his peaceful home. To-night, weary, miserable, bewildered as he had been on going upstairs, distracted by the teasing of his companions, it was not wonderful that he should for once have forgotten the duty ; if he had remembered it, perhaps he would not have had courage to brave the mocking of his heedless associates. The thought came into his mind now, along with thoughts of home, his mother, his sisters, and his little brother, hitherto his one sleeping companion. It was that which gave him the uncomfortable consciousness—the feeling that his mother would be sorry. But perhaps it would not be too late to say his prayers now. He looked round : it was dark, but for a pale ray of moonlight which came through the high window ; and the others were all asleep. Would they wake and see him if he moved ? No—he would not be long ; he thought his mother would tell him it was right, and he would take courage.

He knelt up on the bed, put his hands together, and said the words to himself—shaking all the time, partly with cold, partly with fear of being discovered ; and it must be confessed that most of the poor boy's thoughts, during those few moments, went in anxiety lest Byrd should open his eyes. He need not have been afraid : Byrd had only waited till the others were quiet to say his own prayer ; but Arthur had not known this. Arthur's effort, imperfect as it might be, was a great and a sincere one, made in the simplicity of childlike faith and obedience ; and may we not trust that such efforts, however imperfect, will be accepted ?

No one woke—no human eye saw the lonely little boy at his silent prayer. And when he lay down again beside his sleeping companion he felt less lonely and less frightened. Though he still cried to think how far he was from home, his tears were quieter ones ; and at last they ceased altogether, and he was sleeping as peacefully as if he were in his own little bed.

But he did not know, he could not have imagined, the sorrow of those loving hearts at home. Before his parents had had time to miss him that morning, his cap, found in the river, had been brought to them : they had then ascertained that he was not at school, and the natural conclusion at which they had arrived was that he must have been playing by the river (against which he had often been warned), had fallen in, and been drowned. His father had ridden miles, both up and down the course of the river, to search for his body, but in vain.

And that night, long after he was asleep, his poor mother was sitting beside his little brother Willie, who kept starting up in his bed and crying out about " poor Arthur and the river."

If only he had not loitered on his way to school that morning !

CHAPTER II

THE SONG

ARTHUR slept soundly in spite of his misfortunes —slept until he was awakened by some one shaking his arm.

" Will ! " he said, for the first moment thinking that it was his little brother who was trying to awaken him ; but the face of another Will, his champion of the preceding night, reminded him that he was far from home.

" Get up quickly," said Byrd ; " it is the best counsel I can give you, for Gyles is ill-pleased if we are late."

Arthur was a good boy to get up in the morning generally, and he roused himself at once to obey the friendly warning. But what with his long ride and his flogging the previous day, the poor child felt so stiff and sore all over, that he could scarcely help crying out when he moved. He dressed himself hastily, and shuffled down stairs after William Byrd, presenting, with his neglected appearance, and his uncombed hair hanging about his face, a striking contrast to the bright happy boy that had left Ferry Grange, on his way to school, only the morning before.

Gyles heard him repeat his task first of all. He got through it better than he had ever dared to hope ; and when this was over, the whole class were called to their singing lesson, an hour before breakfast. A weary hour it was, except to the few who, like Byrd, had a turn for music, and were perfect in their parts. Arthur, who was really fond of singing, found that the art, as practised under the eye and hand of the terrible Master Gyles, was very unlike his previous acquaintance therewith, when he had joined in glees with his family at home, or practised the simple plain-song with the boys of the village choir ; for this beautiful and important part of the service of the Church was indeed less neglected in those early times than in some which may be deemed more civilized.

"Sing out, boy, and take pains ! " exclaimed Gyles to Arthur, when they were singing up the scale. "That is not as you sang yestermorn."

What with previous fatigue, fear, and hunger, poor Arthur's voice was so hoarse and tremulous, indeed so unlike its usual self, that perhaps there might be some excuse for the brilliant idea which

suddenly darted into his mind, and which he
seized on as a signal of release.

" Please, sir, I think my voice is broken."

A general roar of laughter burst from the class.
Gyles turned round, sternly commanding silence,
and then addressed Arthur with—

" Let me have no more of thy insolence, or
thou shalt know what it is to have thy head
broken."

Arthur dared make no further reply, but went
on with his task, going through the grand old
" Te Deum " of Merbecke in a most doleful and
plaintive treble, stumbling and making false
notes, mumbling the words, and hanging down
his head like a culprit. Perhaps, even that was
better than singing it as most of the others did,
shouting and gabbling, often with a careless laugh
on their faces, as utterly devoid of all thought and
reverence for the sacred words as though they had
been singing a glee or a ballad. Indeed, they had
never been taught otherwise. To be sure, Master
Gyles was very particular as to time, and tune,
and pronunciation—extremely severe ; during the
course of the lesson he was constantly dealing out
blows and thumps, and Arthur had the diversion
of seeing two of his comrades soundly flogged ;
but there was little to teach the poor boys to
think of the meaning of the words they sang.

Perhaps this story may one day fall into the hands of some little boy who is so happy as to belong to his church choir. If so, I should be glad if it made him think for a moment how different his lot is from that of these choristers of bygone days, though they sang the very same words, and perhaps the very same chants, many of which have been preserved to our time. I should like to remind him how thankful he ought to be that he lives in such far happier days, and that if he allows himself to be careless and irreverent, it is far less excusable, and so far more wrong in him, than it was in those poor children, who had no kind friend or teacher to put them in mind of the holiness of their calling, but were driven to their task by sharp words, blows, and flogging, making it irksome and hateful to them.

After the lesson was over, the boys went to their breakfast, consisting of bread, meat, and small beer. The monotony of the meal was relieved by little squabbles, breaking out from time to time between the boys ; Arthur's neighbours on either side making a point of constantly snatching pieces of food from before him, and giving him their crusts to eat.

Breakfast over, he had another lesson given him to learn by heart, while the rest of the boys went to the task of getting up their parts of a play, which was to be acted shortly. In those days, the children of the Chapel Royal were made, besides their duties in the choir, to perform plays at one of the theatres in London ; and, if one may believe the history of the time, were much applauded as actors.

Before dinner, there was another hour to practise their singing. In this lesson Arthur got on better, though a recurrence of one of his wonted idle fits, towards the conclusion, brought upon him a beating which made him cry all dinner-time.

Some days passed without bringing anything worth recording ; and Arthur, child as he was, began to grow a little reconciled to his new life. Not but that he was very homesick at times, and wondered constantly what his parents thought, and whether they would come to look for him. He little knew that they were mourning for him as dead.

With his companions he got on fairly well. As the youngest of the party he came in for a good deal of teasing, but he was a brave high-spirited little fellow, and held his ground against them manfully, besides having a powerful protector in William Byrd. For a certain friendship and liking had sprung up from the first between

Arthur and this boy, who had been flogged for taking his part, and had helped him through with his difficult exercise. Byrd had, both from seniority and his high position in the school, attained to a kind of leadership among the boys ; and in his presence Arthur was comparatively safe from undue bullying. Arthur did not dislike his work but for the severity of his master. In those days, when even parents were often rough and harsh and indeed unkind to their children, it was not to be expected that masters should be thoughtful or lenient. Thomas Gyles was no exception to the general rule, and his scholars bore him small goodwill.

Arthur liked singing in the Chapel best. There at least he was safe for the moment from his master's rod ; and when he was familiar with the music he really enjoyed his part, and the grand organ-playing of Tallis, or some other " mighty master " of those musical days. His voice which, so far from coming to the untimely end which he had at first desired, was remarkably good, improved much under diligent cultivation ; and though so young he very soon became one of the best singers among the boys, a circumstance which began to excite the jealousy of some of his less gifted seniors.

So time went on, and Arthur fared altogether about as well as his comrades. Under such strict discipline as that of Master Gyles, he was beginning, perforce, to fight against his natural heedlessness, though it brought upon him many floggings before it was in any degree conquered.

But harder days were in store for him. William Byrd was his great stay and helper; and at midsummer William Byrd was going to leave the school, much to the envy of his juniors. He would still reside in London, his father belonging to the Chapel Royal; but would pursue his musical studies solely under his master, Tallis.

" I would I were in thy shoes, Will! " cried Philip Drew, the day before that on which Byrd was to leave. He was a big boy, the next in age to Byrd, but by no means so disposed to be friendly to Arthur. " Thou art lucky to have done with Gyles' rod."

" I wish we were all in Will's shoes," echoed another. " Truly the life we lead here is scarce to be borne, that it is not ! "

" We might as well be dogs," ejaculated a third, who had been the last to smart under the afore-mentioned rod. " I don't believe, if the Queen's Majesty knew all we endure at old Gyles' hands, she would permit it to continue. I 'm sure no one can say we 're justly treated.''

" Justly, quotha! little enough of justice here,'' was the hearty assent of a fourth malcontent. " We 're flogged like brute beasts, whether we do well or ill. I think he gets worse instead of mending.''

I should observe, by the way, that this conversation took place in the afternoon, when the boys were left alone to learn their tasks.

> " Of all the creatures less or mo,
> We little poor boys abide much woe,''

spouted another lad, who had the character amongst his fellows of a turn for verse-making.

" Well done, Johnny Radford, follow it up,'' cried the others. " We 'll get up a petition in the form of a doleful lamentation, and sing it next time we play before Her Majesty.''

" We have a cruel master, I tell you all for true,''

began Radford, encouraged by the popular feeling.

" So cruel as he is, was neither Turk nor Jew,''

struck in William Byrd, with ready wit.

" And oh, say something about his unjust

dealing," entreated the boy who had been last
flogged.

"It availeth us nothing, all our pains——"

"Nay, hush, I have it," said Radford, and he
continued,

" It availeth us no whit to be painful in good deed,
    For there is not one of us but he will make him
        bleed ;
    And because he hath beaten one boy, he will
        beat another,
    And when he hath well whipt one, then will he.
        whip his brother,
    That we, poor silly boys, should abide much
        woe ! "

The applause at this was unbounded.

"Write it down at once, is my counsel," said
Philip Drew, "otherwise we shall forget it ere
it is half made."

"Very well, I will see. Hold thy peace! I
shall have your names in the song, that it may
be more moving."

" Ye might see him whipping Philip, till his body
        was whipped red,
    And when he had beaten Philip, he whipped
        Arthur till he bled—"

"No, no! you shan't say Arthur," indignantly objected that young gentleman, who was just then swinging his lesson-book by one leaf. "I won't be put in."

"Yes, you shall," said Philip; "you're never flogged without reason—which is what can be said of no one else. Go on, Johnny, and give it him well."

"For he sang but a fit or twain, then he could
    sing no farther,
  Wherefore he took a right good rod, and laid
    it well on Arthur,
  That he, poor boy, should endure the more
    woe!"

The audience clapped, stamped, and shouted with delight, all except poor Arthur, who turned very red, in a mixture of anger and shame.

"I won't—I won't have you say that."

"Oh, won't you, young master!—they're the best lines in the whole piece. Write it, Johnny, I say," cried several.

"Give me paper and ink," said Johnny. "Who has a scrap of paper?"

"Here, write in Arthur's book," said Philip, at the same time snatching it up from before him. "There is a fair sheet. Write thy best,

John, that Her Majesty may see what scholars there are amongst us."

" But will Her Majesty see that about me ? " said Arthur in much concern, firmly believing that they were in earnest.

" Of course, of course. Truth and justice ! You know you get more beatings than any of us for idling."

" I 'm sure it isn't true," said the aggrieved Arthur.   " And you 're writing all over my book. Oh, if Master Gyles see it ! "

" See it !—as if we were going to leave it there, thou blockhead ! "

" Then you 'll tear my book, and Master Gyles will be wroth with me—I will have the book, I say."

He had risen to the rescue, but was instantly pinioned by Philip, and had to sit helplessly watching the process of the writing.   The other boys crowded round Radford, inciting him to haste, suggesting and applauding.   In a short time he had written down all that we have quoted, besides some graphic descriptions of Gyles' barbarities, winding up with earnestly expressed hopes, on the part of all his loving pupils, that he might meet speedily with the death he deserved, by hanging.

" Now recite ! " cried the impatient audience.

Radford laid down his pen with an air of great self-complacency, then rose from his seat, and taking the book, began :

" Of all the creatures, less or mo,
  We little poor boys abide much woe ;
  We have a cruel master, I tell you all for true,
  So cruel as he is——"

" Hush ! what 's that ? " suddenly cried one or two of the listeners, starting up, as a confused noise of hooting, yelling, and shouting in the street outside broke upon their ears.

" Let 's away and see ! " and away they all rushed, the grave senior, William Byrd, at their head. A row was a row to schoolboys then as now, and out they darted into the street, where a crowd had collected, hooting and pelting some unfortunate object with mud, sticks, stones— anything that came to hand.

The boys were not long in learning the cause of the uproar. One Master Woolmer, a Papist, had been heard speaking in terms disrespectful to Her Majesty, at a neighbouring tavern, and was being mobbed through the streets by a loyal public.

In the preceding reign, when the Romish

religion was in the ascendant, great persecution
had arisen, and much cruelty had been practised
towards the Reformers, as those young persons
who have read the History of England will
probably be aware. Now, when the reformed
religion had been firmly established, and was
maintained by the Queen herself, it was perhaps
not wonderful that there should be much bitter-
ness of feeling towards the Romanists. I do
not say that this was right, or consistent with
the principles of those who profess our holy faith ;
but the rude mob of London, who on this occasion
were hunting a single, helpless man with every
expression of contempt and insult, were not likely
when their feelings were excited to consider the
right or wrong of their conduct. Neither did
the Chapel boys, who one and all joined in the
uproar for uproar's sake, caring little whom
or what they struck.

They were quickly mingled with the crowd,
shouting and yelling in a way which bid fair
to ruin their voices—if it were not for the untold
amount of exertion that a boy's voice will stand
without being the worse. Not only their voices,
however, were in danger on the present occasion.
Arthur's rash hardy courage had led him into the
thickest of the fray, where he entered into a

personal conflict with a stout waterman's boy about three times his own size. Of course he was knocked down in the twinkling of an eye, and his sturdy antagonist, with his foot upon his chest, was in a position shortly to crush all the breath out of his body, when a strong active form darted to the rescue, and a struggle began over the prostrate Arthur. He was dragged away at last, half insensible, by William Byrd, his generous champion ; and it is to be doubted whether the poor Papist himself, when he got home that night, (if indeed he did ever get home,) was in a more deplorable condition than the youngest of Master Gyles' pupils.

That gentleman had come out to look for his scattered troop, and his countenance was several degrees more wrathful than usual as he met the stragglers coming in one by one, with their muddy garments, black eyes, and bloodstained faces.

" This is fine conduct," exclaimed he ; " Her Majesty's chapel boys, forsooth ! ye have rather the appearance of drunken vagabonds ; mixing yourselves in every street brawl, amid the vilest rabble ! Ye deserve whatever has come upon you, and it shall not be all that ye have to abide."

Here William Byrd, his own countenance presenting a brilliant variety of tints, came up,

E

dragging with him what looked like a walking lump of black mud, with a good many crimson stains about the front of it.

"A notable figure thou dost cut, in sooth, William Byrd!" was his master's greeting. "A comely face thou wilt have to meet Master Tallis to-morrow! Thyself to be foremost in the brawl, instead of maintaining order amongst thy juniors! As to thee," and as he spoke, Gyles shook the hapless Arthur by his muddy collar, till his few remaining wits seemed shaken out of him, "I might have known where to look for thee. Thou shalt not soon forget this. And now, all of ye, to bed, supperless, and the first morsel ye taste to-morrow morn shall be the birch." And with that Master Gyles drove his disreputable-looking flock into the house.

It was well for Arthur that this event took place before William Byrd's departure, as he would not have found such another friend among his comrades, and he sorely needed his friendship now. Byrd carried him upstairs, stripped him of his clothes, all caked together with mud, washed the mire and blood out of his eyes, nose, and mouth, and finally laid the poor little bruised tired body comfortably in bed, all with a kind of rough tenderness, very touching from one boy to another. Arthur was thoroughly exhausted, and almost as soon as his head was on the pillow had forgotten his present and prospective troubles in the deep sleep which such exhaustion brings.

Master Gyles' scholars presented, if truth must be spoken, but a pitiful spectacle when they assembled next morning, with their black eyes, cut faces, and damaged garments. The anticipation of the punishment which awaited them added to their dejection, for they knew well enough that the breakfast of birch was likely to be no idle threat.

The day was ushered in by a grand flogging all round, beginning with Byrd, whom his master dismissed with the following moving address :

" And now, William Byrd, fare thee well ; I wash my hands of thee from henceforth—but let no man say that I have not tried to do my duty by thee."

The others followed in due order, by their ages; Arthur coming last of all, as being the youngest, but by no means entitled to leniency on that account. By the time the castigation was over, it was past the usual hour for breakfast, to which the unfortunate culprits were then allowed to proceed with what appetite they could muster.

E 2

The events of the preceding evening, together with the morning's performance, and Byrd's departure, had been sufficient to drive away all other thoughts from the heads of the boys, and it was not till they were going into the hall to repeat their lessons later in the day, after a rehearsal in the Chapel, that Arthur suddenly gave a great start, and an exclamation, "Oh, the song!"

A look of general dismay seized upon the rest, for all were equally concerned, and knew that the master's wrath would fall upon the whole community if the fact were discovered.

"It's in Arthur's book," cried Philip Drew. "He'll think it's your doing, Arthur; you may just as well let him, because he'll beat you in either case. So, mind you don't deny it."

"But I didn't write it," said Arthur.

"What matters that, simpleton? Don't you see, you may just as well be flogged alone as with all of us—and if you take the credit——"

Here was heard the awful voice of Gyles calling from the hall. The real authors of the poem pressed round Arthur.

"Promise thou wilt not deny it—or be a traitor and a talebearer."

"I won't say what is false," said Arthur sturdily. "I won't tell of you."

"Promise that you will not—or thou shalt rue it."

"I promise," said Arthur. "Don't hold me, Philip."

"Promise that you will not utter our names," said the great cowardly bully, squeezing the little boy's arm till the colour came into his cheeks.

"I have given my word," said Arthur proudly, and they pressed into the hall.

A furtive and anxious glance was cast at the face of Thomas Gyles by each of his pupils as they entered. It wore its usual stern expression, a little increased perhaps by their delay. He evidently had not discovered the lines.

Arthur's turn to repeat his lesson came last, and he sat in an agony of suspense till Gyles took up his book. His task had been but partially learnt (it may be remembered that the lessons had been interrupted, and never finished the day before), and now what little he had known was gone clean out of his bewildered head. He looked up—he looked down—he looked at the others. Their eyes were all upon him.

"Thy wonted idleness, Arthur Savile——"

began Gyles, but just then, as he moved the book, the scribbled page came into view. " Ha! " he suddenly exclaimed, and remained in unfeigned amazement, as he scanned the composition.

It would ill become us to recount the expressions of wrath and hatred levelled at the unlucky Arthur by Gyles, when at length his feelings found vent in words. " So! this is how thy lesson-time is passed—in vile and pestilent slanders against the lawful authorities! Little wonder that thy tasks go unlearnt. ' Lamentation,' quotha! thou shalt have cause to lament for this, or my name is not Thomas Gyles! "

" Sir, I did not write it," said Arthur.

" Not write it ? Well, then, thou hast set on another to write it—it is all one as if thou hadst."

" I did not make it—I did not want it written."

" That is a likely story! At all events thou knowest who hath written it—or wilt thou have the boldness to deny all knowledge thereof ? "

" No, sir," said Arthur bravely ; " I do know."

" Then tell me, candidly, whose work it is."

The other boys looked at him in mute suspense, biting their tongues and holding their breath for anxiety. Would he hold out ?

His answer was undaunted. " I will not tell."

" Will not ? " repeated Gyles, setting his teeth

with rage ; " then thou shalt be flogged until thou
wilt."

The great rod was brought forth again. Arthur
stood firm outwardly, but his heart beat very
fast.   What had he brought upon himself ?

A second severe flogging that day—and it was
very hard to bear a second.   But when Gyles had
exhausted his wrath, Arthur's resolution had not
wavered a whit.

" Wilt thou speak now ? " asked the master.

" I will not."

" Then a like flogging shalt thou endure every
day, until thou speak out."

Arthur said not another word, but walked
away, when he was dismissed, with an air of quiet
determination.

Gyles was as good as his word the next day.
He was excessively irritated both by the poem
itself, which contained too many home truths
to be pleasant to his feelings, and by the firmness
displayed by Arthur.   When he found him still
determined to hold out, he became even more
severe and merciless in his anger.

It must be said in defence of his companions
that they had not expected Arthur's share of the
punishment to be thus protracted.   If William
Byrd had been amongst them, such injustice

would never have been suffered for a day ; but they had begun by allowing the blame to rest on Arthur, and not one of them had courage to come forward now and defend him. Some who, like Philip Drew, were inclined to spite him for his beautiful singing, were wicked enough to rejoice in his suffering : others pitied, even hoped that he would tell ; and perhaps none really imagined that he would sacrifice himself to such an extent for his promise' sake. Boys have easy consciences ; and Arthur's school-fellows persuaded themselves that, after all, he did not perhaps mind the beating so much. If he did, why, it was in his own power, by a single word, to free himself : if not, it did not signify. Old Gyles would give in at last. It was surely better that one should suffer than a whole school.

So they reasoned themselves into the belief that they were not acting otherwise than fairly, in permitting the youngest of their number to suffer daily a punishment that was becoming little short of torture, for a fault in which he had not the smallest share, but of which they were really the originators.

And he never wavered. Arthur Savile had all a schoolboy's horror of a " tell-tale " ; he had, besides, a brave little heart, and, better than all, the secret of true bravery—the fear of doing a false or mean action.

Perhaps it was a pity that he had given the promise so rashly. He was not called upon to sacrifice himself for his careless companions; and his duty was rather to his master in the present instance. But poor Arthur's notions of duty were not clearly defined: he was simply acting up to his highest known standard of truth and honour, at very great cost to himself. It would be well if more did the same.

So a fortnight passed, and Gyles did not relax. He was determined to conquer the boy's obstinacy, and Arthur would give him no other answer than at first.

Some of the younger boys became very uneasy in their minds, Radford amongst the rest. He had more than once begged Arthur to give in; but Arthur met any entreaties of this kind with unwonted surliness, and would listen to no persuasions. The others might perhaps have spoken out before this had it not been for the influence of Philip Drew. Now that Byrd was gone, Philip had most power in the school: he was tyrannical, as cowards always are when in power; he disliked Arthur, and he did not dread the master's anger less for the sight of its endurance. He kept the others quiet by threats and bullying, and Arthur was allowed to suffer on.

Arthur had seemed quite an altered being during the last week or two. Instead of being always ready to run, jump, and play with the others not only in but out of play hours, he was now listless and silent, liking better to steal away by himself than to join their games. They little knew, those thoughtless cowardly boys, the suffering, both mental and bodily, which they had entailed upon that lonely child ; the bitter tears shed in secret when they were sleeping ; the sickening hopes and doubts and fears that chased each other through his young brain.

He was feeling particularly low-spirited one evening. He seemed, even to himself, to be growing so strangely different from what he used to be ; so dull and hardened and uncaring, as if all his senses were being beaten out of him. And indeed it could scarcely be otherwise when all his energies of mind and body were concentrated upon the one great daily effort of endurance.

How long was it to last ? was the question which again and again recurred to his troubled mind. Sometimes he thought he could not hold out any longer ; but then his mind revolted from the idea of turning tell-tale at last, and there was a proud, stubborn spirit in the boy that seemed to gain strength from opposition.

"Arthur, this will not do!" said Radford, after they had gone up to bed on the evening in question. "You must tell to-morrow."

"Yes, indeed, you may," said another younger boy, whose name was Morley, and who had been one of the great promoters of the song-writing. "We never thought of its going on so long. You can't stand it any more."

"It's worse than anything old Gyles has done yet," said Marston, a third. "I declare I'd much rather we were flogged all round, and have done with it. I can't stand its all falling on you."

To all which, and many more persuasive words, Arthur only replied by turning his shoulder upon them with a grunt, but presently began to cry silently.

"It shall not be—it shall not!" cried Radford, in an impulse of virtuous emotion. "You may tell—do you hear? You have our free permission. Do give in, Arthur," and he patted him coaxingly upon the back.

"Go your ways, and hold your peace," said Arthur bluntly.

"Oh, well, if thou art such a cross-grained

knave, do as thou wilt. Take thine own course and abide by it!" And from that moment the boys thought themselves the aggrieved party, and Arthur manifestly in the wrong.

It was on the following day, after they had been singing at the Chapel, that Arthur, as his manner now was, lingered behind the rest. The organ was still playing, and Arthur always liked to listen to it; but to-day he cared very little for the music; he only wished to be alone and quiet. If any of his comrades cared for him really, they would speak up: he did not want their fair words, tempting him to be false to his promise. He sauntered along an empty part of the building, and at last threw himself down on his face at full length on the stone pavement, and sobbed.

He was alone; there was no one to hear him, and he could not help it, even if it was wrong to cry in a church. People went to church to say their prayers, and to be comforted if they were in trouble; he had heard his mother say something like that. Perhaps help would come to him somehow; and then a verse which he had lately been singing came into his head.

" It is He that delivereth me from my cruel enemies, and setteth me up above mine adversaries: Thou shalt rid me from the wicked man."

Arthur felt quite sure that Master Gyles was a wicked man—a cruel enemy ; and that verse seemed to comfort him. Surely, he would not be left in his power always. He would have liked to pray that Master Gyles might leave off beating him ; but he did not quite know how : he was afraid it might be wrong. However, he always thought of that now when he said "Deliver us from evil." Perhaps his early troubles were good for him in this way amongst others, that they taught him to put a little reality into his prayers.

Presently the notes of the organ ceased, and Arthur heard footsteps approaching, and the sound of persons conversing in low tones. They were Master Tallis and his pupil Byrd, as Arthur could tell by their voices. He did not raise his head, though he heard Master Tallis say, as they passed, "One of the singing boys ? "

"Yes, sir," answered the voice of Byrd, "an old friend of mine. Suffer that I have a word or two with him." He paused, while his master proceeded on his way.

"What do you here alone, Arthur ? It is not your wont."

Arthur made no answer, but only pressed his face closer to the flags.

"What has befallen thee, boy? Wilt thou not answer an old friend?"

Still he was silent, and Byrd, changing his tone a little, went on to say, "I can't help wondering how it is, when you have so good a talent, that you should taste the rod so often, Arthur. I heard Gyles commend your singing but yesterday. What does he flog you for?"

"Who told you I'd been flogged?" said Arthur, in a gruff voice.

"Who told me? Why, boy, it is not so long while since I smarted under Gyles' rod that I cannot tell when I see another in like case," replied Byrd, good-humouredly. "Is it the old enemy still—the heedlessness?"

Arthur could not answer this, but sobbed more violently.

"Come, lad, don't stay howling here, unless thou hast a mind to be locked up for the night," said Byrd, taking him by the arm. "Get up and come out with me, and tell me thy troubles by the way."

Arthur did not resist, and rose; but as they reached the door of the Chapel he hung back, and clinging to Byrd, exclaimed, with tears, "I cannot, I cannot go back!"

"How is this?" asked his amazed friend.

"I cannot; he will kill me!" sobbed Arthur, his long-tried fortitude at length breaking down. "I cannot bear it any longer. Oh, Will, take me away!" and his face expressed such real terror that his friend was quite concerned.

"Stop thy tears, boy, and tell me the truth," said Byrd. "If thou art in real distress it may chance I can aid thee. Let me know."

"It is the song—that song that they wrote," said Arthur, at last unable to resist the temptation to unburden his heart to Byrd, who, as a party concerned, certainly had a right to know. "He found it in my book, and he beats me every day. He has flogged me every day for eighteen days. I had six cuts this morning for singing false, and he'll flog me to-night all the same."

"The song—Radford's song—I do not understand this. You had nought to do with the song."

"No; but—but—I promised—they made me promise—not to tell."

Byrd's face, as the facts dawned upon him, might have been a study for a painter. He stopped for a moment as if thunderstruck; then, seizing Arthur by the arm, strode on, without speaking another word, to the school-house.

In at the doorway, into the familiar old hall

he rushed, where he only found the boys assembled at their tasks, Master Gyles being absent. But his indignation was not to be restrained.

"A precious crew ye are, in good sooth, of sneaking cowards! I wonder how much longer you would have held your peace, and seen the innocent suffer for you! A fine pass is this for our school to be come to! Yes, ye may well hang your heads, like traitors as you are. I tell ye that this child here has more worth and more manliness than all of you put together; and there is not one of you that may dare to look an honest fellow in the face. I wish I could lash you all as ye deserve!"

"Master William Byrd," said the grave voice of Thomas Gyles, who had entered unperceived, and had listened in much astonishment to the concluding sentence of this harangue.

"Yes, sir, it is I," said Byrd undauntedly, turning to the master: "I am here to tell you that here hath been a foul and a crying shame— a wicked injustice wrought upon an innocent child. I mean Arthur Savile, who hath been flogged without mercy for a deed of which he is less guilty than any who are here—of which he is entirely innocent, as I can testify."

"He hath been flogged for his obstinacy and

pertinacious insolence," said Gyles sternly. " I know not what tales he may——"

" He hath told no tales ! " burst out Byrd. " I drew from him with difficulty the simple facts, when I found that he was in fear of his life in returning. He gave his word——"

" Master Byrd," said Gyles, with cool displeasure, " I will ask you to conclude this scene. Such interference with the discipline of the boys under my charge is what I will submit to from none but my lawful superiors."

" Hear me once," cried Byrd. " You found, as I am aware, a song in Arthur's play-book——"

" A vile and pestilent libel," interposed Thomas Gyles.

" Let it be what it was, it was written there against Arthur's will and pleasure ; he had neither voice nor part in the making. I, sir, was one of the instigators ; the others I will not spare to make mention of, as they have held their peace so long. John Radford was the principal author ; Philip Drew, Morley, Marston," and he went on to name several others, " all joined in the work. And so far as I can learn, sir, they extorted a promise from Arthur, knowing it would be laid to him first of all, that he would not speak against them. Of his fortitude, Master Gyles, thou hast

F

been the witness. Of them, sir, I can only say that, had I remained in the school, you should not have been an hour ignorant of our part in the matter."

"But we told him he might tell," interposed a timid voice amongst the boys, who were collected together in shame and fear at the upper end of the hall.

"And we said he might say it was his," continued another, no less than that of Philip.

"Ye gave him leave to utter a falsehood—a gracious permission, in sooth!" cried Byrd.

"They shall all receive something for their share in this business," said Thomas Gyles.

"For that, sir," said Byrd, "I must request that you begin with me, as the eldest of the offenders. I have no wish to escape my due deserts. As to the song itself, it was but an idle jest of idle boys, and never intended to come before your eyes. As such, it is surely scarce worth notice ; but the meanness, the dastardly cruelty, of allowing a young child to suffer so long and so greatly, when a word from one of them would have spared him, is a crime that a month's flogging would, in my eyes, scarce expiate. And Arthur's truth and fortitude, methinks, deserve something more than praise."

" The boy has certainly shown firmness in holding to his word," said Gyles, " albeit in a wrong cause, and in defiance of lawful authority ; but he has received a severe chastisement, which may prove salutary in after life."

Gyles then desired the trembling Philip to hand him the rod, under which poor Arthur had suffered so long and so keenly, and to prepare himself for the first infliction ; having declined to accept Byrd's submission.

Arthur, however, who had listened in silent astonishment, not unmixed with apprehension, to the explanation which had been going on, here found courage to speak for the first time, and in behalf of those who had injured him.

" Oh pray, sir, good Master Gyles, whip them not now. I do not deserve to ask any favour, for I have given you much pains and sore trouble ; but I beg you, of your clemency, to spare them. They will never do so again."

" Silence ! " cried Gyles sternly. " They deserve to abide the rod, and from me they shall have their deserts. And thou, Arthur, though thou hast been treacherously dealt with by them, art not faultless : thy rebellion and insolence have but met their reward."

F 2

And Master Gyles was inexorable. Perhaps he had some right on his side. Perhaps, too, he forgot to consider that he would fare ill himself, did he look only for his deserts.

Of the whole lot, perhaps, Philip Drew behaved worst under the castigation, roaring and blubbering like a great coward as he was, under pain not half so severe as he had seen daily inflicted for his sake upon Arthur, who, on the other hand, had learnt to bear his sufferings without screaming—nay, almost without flinching.

In spite of his fortitude, Arthur's long-endured trial met with small acknowledgment from the authors of it. Instead of being thankful to him for doing what not one of them would have done in his case, they felt themselves injured because, forsooth, Arthur had not held out till his master was tired. What was the good of all he had borne, if he was to go and tell Byrd at the end of it, and get them all into trouble ?

But the matter blew over, as all matters, great and small, blow over, in time—not so devoid of consequences, however, as we in our carelessness are prone to think. Arthur's spirits, relieved from the constant strain of endurance, regained their natural vivacity; and long before the outward scars of the rod were healed the memory of his weeks of trouble had been nearly obliterated from his childish mind.

CHAPTER III

THE WHERRY

It was a bright moonlight night in June. The streets and roofs of the great city lay spread out in the white beams, almost as clearly as in the day-time ; and, guided by this light alone, a single small figure was hurrying along the paths leading most directly from one of the great wharves on the river to the house occupied by Master Thomas Gyles and his scholars. London streets were not lighted by lamps in those far-back times ; and if Arthur Savile had not had the bright moon to show him his way he would have fared ill in those dark thoroughfares.

A year had passed since the affair of the song— more than a year since Arthur had been taken from his home to be a chorister in London. Much had happened to him in that time, both for good and for evil. Some of his old failings had been driven out of him by Gyles' rod ; but, on the other hand, his companions taught him and coerced him to do many things which he had been brought up to think wrong, and which led him into trouble either outward or inward—frequently both.

With his work he certainly got on well. His beautiful singing had become famous among the musicians attached to the Chapel Royal ; and Master Tallis, with whom he was an especial favourite, had bestowed upon him the name of the Golden Treble, by which name he was soon generally spoken of by the men of the choir, on account of the sweetness of his voice. It had also attracted the notice and won for him the favour of the Queen herself ; and of all the boys, he was the most frequently required to sing in her presence.

It would be strange, perhaps, if so much notice had not made him a little vain. It met, however, with a powerful counteracting influence in the unflagging severity of Master Gyles, and the behaviour of the other boys, with whom he was by no means a favourite, though they contrived to make him a catspaw on more occasions than we have time to record.

But what was he doing out here in the streets at midnight ?—Certainly no errand for Master Gyles. Let us follow him.

His year of London life had taught him how to find his way about ; for he never hesitated, but threaded his course through street and lane, till he arrived at the school-house. Here, instead of entering by the door, he climbed a low wall fencing in a court at the back. From the top of the wall Arthur, with monkey-like agility, stepped upon a narrow ledge of brickwork against the house, and slid himself along it till he stood under a window which he could just reach by stretching up, and against which he gave a scarcely perceptible tap with his finger. It was instantly unclosed, and, seizing the window-sill with his hands, Arthur pulled himself up, and scrambled through the opening like a cat. He dropped safely on the floor of the long hall within, where Morley was waiting for him.

" Is it all right ? " was the whispered question of this boy.

" Ay," returned Arthur ; " to-morrow afternoon, at two of the clock."

" That is well." And the two stole noiselessly up to the dormitory, whose occupants were in a state of much excitement.

What were they plotting that required this midnight expedition, these perilous manners of entrance and exit ? The facts were these : for some time past the minds of the boys had been set upon a boating excursion on the river—a thing, of course, which would have excited the utmost anger of Master Gyles had he had the slightest conception of such a scheme. They had none of them any notion of managing a boat ; but they had once or twice procured a stolen row in a wherry ; and, having come home without serious misfortune, by this time thought themselves perfectly competent to undertake the responsibility. Arthur, who being the youngest was always forced to take the service of difficulty and danger, had on this night been sent out to make the final arrangements with the Thames waterman of whom they had agreed to hire the boat.

The influence of Philip Drew over the rest of the boys had become in the last year more complete and baneful than before. Radford, the next in age to him, was not an ill-disposed boy, but easily led by example ; and as that example was good or bad, so was his conduct. And now that William Byrd was no longer there to make head against the tyrant, the younger boys were either drawn or forced into mischief, according to their dispositions, at his will and pleasure.

Arthur had, perhaps, of all his subjects, given him the most trouble. Arthur was heedless, and

easily led into feats of skill and daring; but
though he might have become less conscientious
than of yore, his companions had never been able
to make him utter a direct falsehood to serve
them. Yet he was a good-tempered, unselfish
little slave, and, with his curious mixture of
persuasibility and sturdy honesty, possessed
useful qualities for a scapegoat. He was very
bold and active, too, venturing himself for the
very fun of the thing into dangers such as Drew
and his more timid associates would shrink from.

This night's business successfully accomplished,
the boys settled themselves in bed; but it was
long before any of them could sleep. Arthur
especially was much excited by the prospects of
the morrow. A stolen pleasure had charms for
him still, as on the day when Master Gyles had
first offered him a ride. But his conscience
was not quite easy yet about such matters, as his
disturbed slumbers, when he did fall asleep,
might have testified.

Suddenly, after long tossing, and incoherent
rambling talk, Arthur started up in his bed with
a cry that sounded through the room and aroused
his companions. "Oh! help—help! Oh! where
is the boat?"

Drew, who was nearest to him, raised his

head with an impatient exclamation, and bade
him be quiet ; but Arthur's eyes were shut, though
he sat up and spread out his hands. Drew
seized him and shook him roughly by the arm.

" Philip—oh ! don't—oh ! is it you ? " cried
Arthur, waking. " Are you safe ? Oh ! was it
all a dream ? I thought the boat upset."

" I 'll upset you, you little dreaming jackass ! "
said Philip angrily, " waking us all out of our
first sleep with your follies."

" Oh, but it was so fearful ! Methought we
were in the water struggling, and then I saw you
all stretched out, and white and dead, and your
hair straight. Oh, Philip, let us not go ! "

" If ever I heard ! " began Philip, with a
mocking laugh, to hide whatever unpleasant
feelings might have been raised by Arthur's
words. " If you don't hold your fool's tongue and
lie down this instant, I 'll give you something
to stop your dreaming, and your screaming
too ! "

Arthur cowered down in bed, silenced, but
quivering all over and his teeth chattering with
nervous terror, very unlike his usual stouthearted-
ness. The fear was infectious.

" Perchance it was an omen," whispered
Marston to Morley. " I say, Arthur," he

continued timidly, stretching over towards him," didst thou dream anything about me ? "

" I don't know—I can't remember," was the answer, also in a whisper. " I only saw Philip plain—he pushed me away, and then—I saw him again—drowned." The last words were lost in a convulsive shudder.

" Do not let us speak of it," said Morley. " Dreams are nought. Go to sleep and forget it."

They did go to sleep at last, and when they woke again in the morning, the impression caused by the dream had considerably lessened. Arthur indeed was very much ashamed of his fear in the daylight ; he expected Philip and the rest to rally him about it. But they did not allude to the subject—a sure proof that the vague awed feeling was lurking still at the bottom of their hearts.

Very little of the boys' attention was given to their tasks that morning. After their dinner, when all of them were assembled in the hall, Master Gyles called Philip away with him privately. Presently Philip returned with a peculiar expression of countenance.

" Master Gyles hath notified to me," he began, " that it is his will and pleasure to be absent this afternoon, and to lock up us, his scholars, to our tasks in the hall, saving Arthur

Savile, whom he is pleased to command to accompany him."

A blank look of dismay fell upon all the faces, especially upon that of Arthur, at the conclusion of the speech.

" We want him to steer—we can't do without him," cried several boys.

" A thought strikes me," said Philip. " Arthur can be seized with a sudden sickness—I will tell Master Gyles he cannot move—you go and lie down there, Arthur."

" But—but," said Arthur, with a struggle for conscientiousness, " that is a lie."

" Do you wish it to be true, knave ? " said Philip, throwing him down on the ground with a violence that almost stunned him, and following it up with a tremendous thump. " There, then," and the next moment he was gone. Almost before Arthur had recovered his senses Drew had returned, saying, " Master Gyles says Morley is to go."

Out went Morley's under lip, and he frowned. " I can steer just as well as Arthur, I am certain."

" I 'll go, if Master Gyles will have me," interposed Marston, the boy who had been alarmed most by Arthur's dream. " I don't care so much for the boating."

"No! no! Morley's heaviest. You be off, Morley!" shouted a chorus; "nobody wants you." And he was hooted out of the room; not however before Arthur, in a spirit of defiance as much as truthfulness, lifted up his head and called out from the floor, "I am not sick, though."

Half a dozen boys were upon him directly, almost crushing his prostrate form with their weight. Not that, as might have been thought from their anxiety to keep him, they cared for his pleasure in the expedition; but he was the lightest of their party, and his previous acquaintance with a river at his own home had given him some notion of steering a boat—no very definite notion, but still one on which he was fond of enlarging. None of the other boys had had any kind of practice in this matter.

When Gyles had left the house, and they had heard the door carefully bolted, Arthur's captors released him, and bade him get up and climb out of the window first. But Arthur, for once in his life, was put out; first, because they had told a lie about him—secondly, because they had made him submit by main force.

"I won't get up! I won't steer you!"

"Ha!" cried Philip, springing forward, "I'll soon settle thy reckoning in that matter."

He seized Arthur by both arms, and raised him up forcibly, saying, as he held him securely, " Now, look ye here, Master Arthur Savile ; I 'm master this afternoon, and I know where the big rod is kept. If thou wilt not obey me without another word, I will flog thee till Gyles comes home, and leave him to finish thee."

Arthur did not quite care to brave this. The disgrace of being beaten by Philip was not to be suffered ; besides which, his resistance now was based upon sullenness and offended pride, not upon a sense of right : so of course it had no endurance. And after all he *did* very much want to go on the river ; and he had tampered too long with his conscience, he had too often ventured near the boundary-line between truth and falsehood, to feel very uneasy now. He quieted any little scruples that yet remained by saying to himself that it was all Philip's doing.

So he got up, and led the way by climbing out at the window, which had been his way out on his midnight errands. The others followed, but with less agility, and Radford got a tumble and a bruised shoulder, which made him cross. Spite of this, however, the boys reached the river side by the hour appointed without interruption or mishap. There was the boat in readiness—a tempting sight as it danced gently upon the clear river—for the Thames was a clear pure river in those days, even in London, and its bright surface, sparkling in the sun, was tempting to others besides the Chapel boys for an excursion on that fair summer day.

Shouting, laughing, pushing, squabbling, the party plunged one after another into the boat, making it rock and lurch alarmingly, and provoking many a jest and a caution from lookers-on ; many a prophecy, too, as they finally shoved off, that they would come to harm ere long.

It looked like it, certainly. Half of the rowers had not the smallest idea of handling an oar, still less of keeping anything like time with each other in their strokes ; consequently, the oars clashed together, crossed, splashed, did anything, in short, but propel the boat. Then, of course, they could not expect to find themselves sole occupants of the river, and many were the taunts, oaths, and execrations levelled at them by indignant watermen with whom they came in contact. Some hit at them with oars, or threatened to duck them ; while, furious as they were at the insults, they were powerless to make any return, it being fully as much as they could do to keep themselves and their craft above water.

Of course, whatever mischances occurred were laid by each to the other, so that the party in the boat was by no means an harmonious one. Arthur came in for his due share of abuse. It was convenient for the rowers to lay the blame of their unskilfulness upon the steersman : he, on his side, laughed at their unpractised efforts, and gave back taunt for taunt.

" I 've dropped my oar," cried Radford at last.

" And I 'm so tired of rowing," said another. " I wish I might steer ; I could do it a great deal better than that fool Arthur."

" Ho, ho, ho ! I would fain see you steer ! " retorted Arthur, laughing. " But see, what a concourse of people on yonder bank ! What can they be assembled there for ? "

Philip, and several of the rowers, turned round to look. The banks of the river, on either side, were thronged with people ; looking out evidently for something, as they strained their eyes in the opposite direction to that whence the boys had come.

Strains of music in the distance broke upon their ear, now swelling nearer and nearer : then came in sight a great barge, decorated with flags streaming in the wind. The spectators pressed

G

closer and closer to the water's edge, and at the same moment the truth flashed upon the boys, " It is the Queen ! "

All ways went the oars, as one after the other of the rowers stood up and turned round to have a better view. Arthur let go the tiller, and stood up with the rest. Up and down, round and round went the boat. The boys were hooted, shouted at, shoved aside by all who came in contact with them ; they seemed utterly to have lost their wits.

" Oh, see ! " said Arthur presently. " There is the Queen's Majesty herself, and the great lords, and oh ! if there is not Master Tallis, speaking to her."

" And that,—why, surely," cried Marston timidly, " that is Master Gyles. Oh, what will become of us ? "

" Gyles ! Gyles, quotha ! " exclaimed Philip angrily. " Your eyes see Gyles in every waterman's wherry. A likely story ! "

" It is Gyles, of a surety," said Arthur, looking in the direction in which Marston pointed. " See, Philip, now he speaks with Master Tallis. And there is Morley ; don't you see him now ? "

" Sit down, and steer, blockhead," said Philip, pushing him into his seat violently. " Do you wish to run Her Majesty down ? "

Perhaps Philip thought this the least humiliating way of putting their danger ; perhaps too he considered his own craft as the more considerable of the two. Certainly, it took apparently far more to manage than the great majestic barge, gliding smoothly along its shining way.

Nearer and nearer it came : the boys could distinguish the terrible features of Master Gyles distinctly, and at him they looked in most concern, in spite of the presence of the Queen and some of the highest noblemen of the court. And no doubt these august personages, with Master Tallis and the rest of the company, musical and non-musical, were not a little astonished when they saw the unfortunate little boat rocking in the Royal pathway, with the crew of choristers, and Golden Treble at the stern.

They made one desperate effort to save their credit ; but of the three oars which remained at their disposal not one would go the right way. Arthur, in his bewilderment, turned the tiller precisely as he should not have done : the head of the boat struck the Royal barge, and was immediately upset. The next moment the water was covered with small struggling figures ; the air rang with their cries.

Arthur had clung at first to a portion of the boat,

and it was like the horrible realization of his
dream when he felt his grasp forcibly unloosed,
and his clutching hands pushed away. He
saw not by whom, for everything seemed confused
and sinking around him. But in that moment of
terror and bewilderment, his thoughts and his
sense of danger were clear and distinct ; and
perhaps his first and most painful feeling was,
that he should never see his parents, his little
brother and sisters, again. Never in this life ;
but Arthur had been taught that there is a life
beyond, though in his young carelessness he had
given little thought to it. It seemed very near
now ! And then, so many naughty things that
he had said and done came back to his recollection, things forgotten long ago ; and in the last
year, the many instances in which he had given
way to his companions, in what at the time
seemed but such trifling matters of conscience, and
yet, looked at on the verge of that other life,
were so great : the slight deviations from truth,
which had begun to weaken his firmness, rose up
in his mind too, the reasons, the excuses given
for them, seeming so worthless now : oh ! if he
could once live over again his life, he would suffer
anything rather than do wrong. How such
thoughts can be gathered into a few short moments

none can say : it is amongst the mysteries of our
nature ; but that they may be, is an established
fact. And Arthur saw the sun shining, the bright
sky above him, the faces in the barge and on the
bank, all things belonging to the life from which
he was being so suddenly torn away : he was
dying, yet so fearfully conscious and alive !
Suddenly some one seized hold of him, but it
was with a sinking, not a saving grasp ; and
a voice, which he knew to be that of Marston,
cried " Save me ! " with a ringing, piercing cry.
He clutched, too, at the struggling figure near him,
felt himself borne down ; and then no sensation
remained but a rushing, ringing sound in his head
and ears, like the ringing of bells, and in his fancy
it seemed the chimes, not of London, but of the
bells in his old village church at home, pealing
as they used to do on high festivals, in his early
days. It was the last sensation of which he was
conscious.

But in the mean time, those around were not
backward in their exertions to save the children.
There were plenty of boats at hand. Philip Drew
had never left his hold on the overturned craft
when he had once seized it : in his cruel selfish-
ness he had pushed away those who were clinging around him. He was the first picked up.

Radford was rescued almost at the same time. But the confusion, and the number who were simultaneously in need of help, created some delay, and Arthur, in the grasp of the sinking Marston, had been carried further than the rest, and had now disappeared. Master Gyles, in great alarm and agitation at the danger of his pupils, had sprung into a small boat, and with his keen eyes was now scanning every part of the surface of the water, watching for the reappearance of those two.   Little as he might love Arthur, he did not want to lose the Golden Treble.

Presently they rose, but further still from the boats, which had gathered in one part of the river.   One boy appeared quite insensible, the other, they could not see which, struggled faintly. Just then a figure darted quickly across two barges, which were lying together by one of the banks, and plunged into the water : a strong active young figure, though not that of a full-grown man ; but a brave and practised swimmer. He made towards the spot where the two boys, locked together in a drowning grasp, had reappeared, seized the collar of one of them, raised his head above the water, and, dragging them both with him, swam up to the nearest boat, which received them, amidst the applause of the spectators.

Those two were the last to be taken out of the
river.

When Arthur at length returned to consciousness he was lying on one of the pallets in Master
Gyles' dormitory. At first he was only sensible
of a confused buzz of voices ; then he saw a light,
for it was late in the evening, and was aware of the
face of William Byrd bending over him, and
heard him say, " He is coming to, Master Gyles
—he is safe."

Then some one lifted him up, and poured some
kind of warm drink down his throat. That
revived him a little, and after one or two
efforts he whispered, " Will, is it true—are we
safe ? "

" Safe, yes," was the answer; " you'll be all
right now."

" But the boat—the others—it upset," then,
in a low, shuddering voice, " are they all—is
Philip safe ? "

" Philip is safe. All are saved except poor
Marston."

" Marston," repeated Arthur, " he held by me ;
is he drowned ? "

" He is," replied Byrd, " he was dead when
they took him out of the water. We thought you
were dead too."

" But I 'm not. Oh, won't poor Marston come to life again ? have they tried ? "

" Yes, they tried. It was of no avail. But now, Arthur, speak no more at present. It is better for thee to sleep."

Arthur was silent. He felt exhausted in body, but his mind was fully awake to the shock. Marston, with whom he had played, and quarrelled, and laughed, and sung ; Marston, a boy like himself, only a year older ; Marston, who had but that morning been alive and in health, like the rest, was lying cold, and stiff, and dead, as Arthur had seen Philip in his strange dream. Marston had clung to him in their moment of peril ; they had sunk and risen together ; but Arthur had been saved, and Marston drowned. It might have been the reverse. What would have become of thoughtless, heedless Arthur then ?

" Who picked me out of the river ? " he asked presently.

" Dost thou ask that, knave ? " said the voice of Gyles, who just then approached his bed ; " it was thy good friend here, Will Byrd, who perilled himself to save thy worthless life. But for him thou wouldst not be alive now, to be a plague and a care to thy masters. But thou shalt not soon forget thy water excursion," and with that he passed on.

"Was it you indeed, Will?" said Arthur, "were you in Her Majesty's barge?"

"I? no; how should I be? I was on the river bank, looking to see Her Majesty pass. I had watched you for some while."

"But Master Gyles and Morley, did I not see them in Her Majesty's company?"

"Surely," replied Byrd. "Some of the lords and gentlemen of the court had set their minds on a musical party, for Her Majesty's diversion, on the water. That was why they sent to Master Gyles to bring a singing boy. I thought it had been you."

"They made me feign sick," said honest Arthur. "They wanted me to steer." And then, changing his tone to a lower, he went on, "Marston was the most afraid of my dream. Think ye, Will, that it was an evil presage?"

"I know nought of thy dream, boy."

"It was Philip who was drowned in my dream; is not that strange? But still, I think it was an omen."

"Maybe," said Byrd quietly.

In those days there was far more superstition and credulity, even amongst the well educated, than exists at present, and men of sense and courage were not ashamed to confess their belief in omens and presages. Therefore Byrd's cool assent to Arthur's suggestion is no matter of wonder.

Who shall say that he was altogether wrong ? If not an omen, might not the strong impression, the vague, insurmountable awe have been permitted as a warning to the careless boys against the stolen and forbidden pleasure which, wilfully persisted in, caused the sudden and untimely death of one of their number ?

CHAPTER IV

THE REHEARSAL

MASTER Gyles kept his word. He administered
to the unlucky young boatmen such a flogging
as they did not soon forget—by no means excusing
the Golden Treble, when he was sufficiently
recovered. He was excessively enraged and
mortified that his scholars, whom he prided himself upon keeping in such strict discipline, should
have thus disgraced themselves in the sight of the
Queen and her court: that the life of one of them
should have been thereby lost (and it was a loss
not easily to be supplied at once, for Marston was
the best second treble in the choir, and an intelli-
gent boy) was sufficiently irritating.

Then there was the boat to pay for. Amongst
themselves the boys had scraped together enough
money to pay for its hire, but on the day following
that on which the accident took place, a stout
wherryman appeared at Master Gyles' door,
demanding damages, and payment for the lost

oars. At first Gyles was ready to refuse to pay, but finding that his scholars had really no more money, and deeming that it ill became his dignity to quarrel with the man, he delivered over the price he demanded, mentally vowing to take it out of the unfortunate boys, which he did by blows and short allowance at meals.

Poor Arthur came off worst of all, both with his master and his companions. The latter were pleased to lay all the blame of the accident upon him and his steering, while Philip Drew spited him for ever about his dream, as if poor Arthur could have helped that. He found that whatever trouble he took, whatever danger he braved for this tyrant, he got no thanks, but was worse treated than the rest.

But time passed, and all things went on after a while as before. Marston's place had been filled by another boy, by name Etheridge. He was nearly a year older than Arthur ; but, as a new-comer, and strange to his work, Arthur took to patronizing him, and pouring forth terrible stories of Gyles for his delectation, as his companions had formerly done by him. Poor Etheridge was not so stout-hearted as Arthur had been, and when Arthur saw how evidently he quailed under the prospects opening before him, he felt a little conscience-smitten and sorry for what he had said. But it was too late when the mischief was done.

On one occasion, after Etheridge's first flogging, when he was in much tribulation, Arthur took upon himself to console him, assuming the tone and almost the words used by William Byrd when on the point of leaving the choir: " Ah, you will get used to it in time. I was just like you once ; but it 's worse for you, of course ; and I don't care about old Gyles as I used."

" Ha, young master, don't you ? " and a rough hand seized Arthur's glossy brown curls, while another pulled his ear, till he was forced to make a most wonderful grimace to keep himself from crying, " I 'll Gyles thee, with thy rebellious impudence ; is 't not enough to be insolent thyself, but thou must egg on thy fellows to disregard of authority ? Take that, and that ! "

When Arthur's cheeks were duly made to tingle, Master Gyles unclosed the book which he had been using as a weapon, having nothing else at hand, and called his troop to order and attention.

" Ye will be required to get up a new Interlude this season, whereof the title is ' The Pilgrimage of Pleasure.' There are eight personages, and the parts are cast as follows :

" Pleasure, the Prologue speaker, is the part assigned to Thomas Morley ; Youth, Philip Drew ; Vain Delight, Arthur Savile " (Arthur gave a little jump on hearing his name, for he had never yet acted, his bad memory for learning by heart being an insuperable obstacle) ; " Sapience, Edward Wilton ; Life, Thomas Fleming ; Death, Francis Etheridge ; Gluttony, the Vice, John Radford ; and Discretion, Edmund Beaton. I will leave the book with you," ended Master Gyles, " and ye will do well to look over your parts at once, and commit as much as ye may to memory."

So saying, he left the hall, and the boys immediately pounced upon the play-book. Arthur especially was greatly excited, having often wished to play.

" Vanity, Vain Delight, Master Gyles said I was to be ! I am so glad. Let me see, Philip ; I will have the book," and a scuffle immediately ensued, to the no small danger of the work in question.

" Let me see my part. Oh, I hope it is not over-long ! "

" Keep off, will you ? your part isn't the first."

"Where does mine begin, Philip? you're hiding it all."

"You'll tear the book, and catch a sound flogging!"

"Give it me, I say—I'm Pleasure and Prologue speaker, and I *will* have it first," said Morley.

"I dare say!" retorted Philip. "My part is the principal of the whole thing, and if you think I'm going——"

"Master Gyles will find we have done nothing——" put in the meeker voice of Etheridge.

"Hold thy peace, fool! There, Morley, take thy worthless part. Thou dost not come in after the first."

"Me! but I'm Pleasure, and the thing is called 'The Pilgrimage——'"

"Ha! here entereth Vain Delight," cried Arthur, who at length contrived to snatch the book over Morley's shoulder. "'Here entereth Vain Delight, with a hawk on her wrist, and singeth'— 'her,' that must be a mistake! I'm not going to be a woman!"

"Ho, aren't you?" said Philip, laughing. "Read the part, and see. For what dost thou take Vain Delight?"

Arthur glanced down the page, his countenance falling visibly, as he was aware of seven stanzas of song to begin with. " I 'm sure I never can learn all this—such fool's nonsense, too ! "

" Read it, I say," said Philip, delighted with an opportunity of teazing him.

Arthur, with a mixture of curiosity and reluctance, obeyed. The song with which his part began, and which we will give at length, was as follows :

> " I am mickle of might,
> I am seemly of sight,
> My name is Vain Delight,
>   If ye would know :
> I am full fair and bright,
> I am both red and white,
> I live in summer's sight,
>   Singing evermo.
> Though I be but small,
> I bind men's bodies all,
> A great queen men do me call
>   In landes where I go.
>
> "All times of the year
> I make right lusty cheer,
> Great joy I have to fere [1]
>   Withouten measure.
> I am ruddy as flame
> For joy and nothing for shame,
> I am called by my name,
>   Very perfect Pleasure.

[1] Companion.

The sun and the starry light,
The day and the blind night,
Feed me with their delight,
 And all their treasure.

" I am the goodliest thing
 That ye shall see this spring,
 There is no manner king
  So great as I.
Amonges the noble sheaves
And under the fair great leaves
My sweet singing cleaves.
 As I go thereby,
Whosoever it hears
It cleaveth to his ears,
It taketh away his tears,
 Till that he die.

" I have a right good note
 In my little sweetè throat;
Whoso it heareth, I wot,
  He shall worship me.
I have a little bird,
It speaketh never a word;
But when it hath me heard,
 Glad will it be.
I bear it on mine hand,
To hunt in summer land,
From green grass to the low sand
 And the sweetè sea.

H

" Where it seeth that it liketh
It crieth Ho ! and striketh ;
It plucketh and piketh
   Both with beak and with feet.
Certes, I you say,
You shall see if I may
A great heron it will slay,
   And all to-bete.
Lo, it cometh, my sweeting,
With flyting and with fleeting,
It is right fain of greeting
   With its hood sweet.

" The sea is full sweet, and green,
Thereas no wind hath been :
I am lady and queen
   Both by sea and by land.
Above mine head I bear
A crown of rubies fair,
And good gold upon mine hair
   And on mine hand.
Wheresoever I pass
There springeth blossom and grass ;
Whereas the dry ground was
   Red new roses stand.

" I am so noble a queen
I have right little teen,[1]
I wear goodly samite green,
   Fresh flowers and red.

[1] Sorrow.

No man so sad there is
But if I will him kiss
With my good sweet lips, I wis
He shall well be sped.
Whoso that will me see
He shall have great joy of me,
And merry man shall he be
Till he be dead."

I think few boys of Arthur's age and peculiar inaptitude for learning by heart, but would be dismayed at being told to commit these seven stanzas to memory as a beginning to his part. But at first Arthur's tone was that of indignation, at having been deceived as to the character he was to assume. He broke out into numberless protestations, violent abuse of the words, the character, the play—he *was not* going to make a fool of himself, whatever old Gyles might say ! Philip and the rest laughed heartily, and, with their jests and taunts, added tenfold to his misery.

" An excellent Vain Delight he will make, of a surety ! Can't you see him mincing in his ruff, with the ' good gold ' on his head ? "

" ' Red and white,' forsooth ! It 's all red, now. Come, cool down a little, sweet Mistress Vain Delight—or thou wilt be in danger of uttering falsehoods."

"So! thou hast a 'right good note '—let us hear it. Pity but we can't get in ' Golden Treble '—I 'll ask Gyles——"

"Nay, I 'll do that for him," interposed the ready verse-maker, Radford.

> "'I am so sweet and small,
> "Golden Treble" men do me call ;
> Whoso shall hear me squall——''"

Here Arthur's sturdy fist, aimed exactly between his eyes, checked the poet's eloquence. Radford was upon him directly, returning the blow with interest, and he being much the bigger Arthur came off but badly. When that scuffle had subsided, and Arthur had picked himself up, Philip placed the book, open at the entrance of Vain Delight, in his hands, saying, with a provoking tone of condescension : "Now, lad, in consideration for thy tender years, and thy slowness of comprehension, and thy daintiness, thou shalt have the first turn in learning. Thy first play, and all—we must have pity upon our sweeting."

"Did he never act before?" inquired Etheridge. "Methought he had been here a long time."

"Ah, yes," replied Philip confidentially,

" but you see he is dull of learning; and then
Marston—that's the knave who was drowned
before you came—he took all those kind of parts.
It 's only because we 're so hard put to it, that
Master Gyles has given it to him—there isn't
another small and dainty enough. Fine work
he'll have to get it into his addled brain. Look,
look ! " he suddenly lowered his tone, and nudging
Etheridge's arm, pointed towards Arthur.

For Arthur was sitting in his old listless
attitude, with his elbows on the table, the book
before him : his square forehead drawn into a
set frown, his under lip thrust out and quivering,
his face indeed " ruddy as flame," though for
something else than joy ; and the long restrained
tears slowly gathering in his great brown eyes.

" Look, look at him, Etheridge ! " continued
the tormentor. " That 's he that doesn't mind
anything now—that doesn't care for old Gyles and
his rod—no, not a whit : it 's only a song makes
him cry."

" Crying for a song ! " said Etheridge, who had
something of the quiet bully in his nature, and
finding himself backed by Philip felt bolder than
usual : " well, I wouldn't cry for a song."

But this was more than Arthur could stand.
He was used to mockery from Philip ; but that

Etheridge, whom he had patronized—Etheridge, the new-comer, should insult him too, was not to be suffered. He threw down the book, flew at Etheridge, and struck him.

" Follow it up ! " cried Philip, and a battle began. Etheridge was bigger than Arthur, but not nearly so active or so used to fighting, and after a sharp struggle, the future Death was stretched on the ground, with Vain Delight kicking, stamping on, and pummelling his prostrate form. In the midst of the scuffle, Master Gyles returned.

Imagine his feelings when he saw the confusion, the book torn, and one of his chief actors with a tremendous black eye, threatening to be a permanent disfigurement !

The end of it was that the combatants received a sound flogging at the hands of that indefatigable master ; and Arthur, somewhat tamed, fell to perusing the hateful lines, with much the same feelings as on that unhappy night when he had first tasted Gyles' rod. Only he had no William Byrd to come to his relief now.

His one consolation, when he found that there was no backing-out of his part, was the hawk which, as Vain Delight, he was to carry on his wrist. This bird was given into his charge that he might tame it, and accustom it to be with him ; but it was a sad hindrance to his learning.

Behold him, one fine morning, with this important personage fastened upon his wrist, hopelessly attempting to con his lesson, between the bird's constant pecking and a spirited colloquy between Life and Youth, who were rehearsing their parts together. For six days had poor Arthur been vainly trying to learn his song, and had advanced no farther than the sixth stanza, in the middle of which he invariably relapsed into some verses belonging of right to Gluttony, but which Radford (in supreme contentment with his part, and the prospect of being padded out to a comfortable and portly figure with cushions) was constantly reciting, and which had somehow or other obstinately fixed themselves in Arthur's perverse memory.

" I wish you wouldn't go on so, aloud ! " he said at length, looking up with his piteous perplexed face. " How is one to learn ? "

" As thy betters do," said Philip, " and besides, all the reciting in the world hinders thee not from coaxing thy sweet bird, which is all thou dost."

" Ah, yes ! " joined in Etheridge, who just now entered, " 'tis all very well for those who have nought to think of but mincing and looking pretty. I wish my luck was as great," he added, affecting an injured air.

" I wish," began Arthur in spiteful earnest, " that you just had to learn this fool's song with all the rest shouting at you. Ah, ah, ah ! " he broke off suddenly, for the hawk was certainly acting up to its character, " plucking and pyking " its master's hand in good earnest. " Let go, thou cross-grained fowl, let go, I say ! "

Etheridge laughed heartily. " List to the dainty dame," he cried ; " which is worse, the hawk's beak or Gyles' rod ? "

" Try," said Arthur, goaded into real maliciousness ; and getting up, he unfastened the hawk's jesses, which secured it an unwilling captive to his wrist, endeavouring to make it attack Etheridge. The latter retreated backwards. Arthur gave the hawk a push towards him, but with a shrill, angry cry, it spread its wings, and flew high up among the dark beams of the hall.

Arthur instantly scrambled upon the table, shouting and making demonstrations more likely to scare away a tame hawk than to entice back a half-wild one. It was hopeless to think of reaching it ; and, after sailing once or twice round the hall, it finally made its escape through one of the high lattices which stood open.

Arthur and Etheridge looked at each other in blank dismay.

" There, ye have done it," exclaimed Philip. " Perhaps now ye will be content."

" Say ' thou,' not ' ye,' " said Etheridge ; " I have nought to do with it. Why, Arthur— whither is he off and away ? "

For Arthur had scrambled out of the window in his often-practised way, and was now rushing across the court in vain pursuit. The hawk was sailing away high over the roofs of the houses. Arthur rushed wildly on, gazing after it, till he stumbled against a pedestrian, whom he had not seen in his headlong run, but who turned out to be William Byrd, on his way to the Chapel.

" Why, how now, Arthur Savile ? "

" Oh, Byrd, the hawk ! " was all panting Arthur could say, and it was some time before his sympathizing friend could understand the history of his troubles. When he at length paused in the narration, Byrd said, " Well, boy, thou art in an unlucky case, truly, but my counsel to thee is to make known the loss at once, and I will also tell all whom I may meet, that if any of them should capture the hawk, it may be restored without delay. And now I must not linger. I wish you well out of it," and he passed quickly on.

Arthur stood for a moment looking after him, envying his emancipation from Gyles, and general immunity from scrapes. He wished he could have had Byrd to go home with him. But it was of no use wishing, so he turned reluctantly towards the house, feeling as much dread of Master Gyles' anger as was compatible with his sturdy careless nature.

Master Gyles was in the hall, and had of course heard the story from the others. It was a terribly angry face that met poor Arthur as he entered. Arthur had often seen his master in a rage, but perhaps never had he beheld him so awful as now. He was positively scarcely able to speak for passion, and when he did find utterance, his language was very violent indeed.

Arthur was quite beyond making excuses or expressing sorrow. He trembled silently before his master's wrath, and awaited the infliction of the rod with apparent indifference, while Gyles swore to flog him within an inch of his worthless life. Then he began in good earnest.

After flogging the boy till he was tired, Master

Gyles laid down his rod, and produced a strong cord, with which he bound Arthur's hands tightly together behind his back, and bidding him follow, walked up the stairs. Arrived at the top, he took out a rusty old key, and unlocked a door in the wainscoted wall, of the existence of which Arthur had never till now been aware. Within was a very narrow, dark closet. Without a single word, Gyles thrust the boy into it, giving him a violent push, which, as his hands were tied, threw him down helplessly upon his face. Then he shut the door, and turned the key with a hopeless, grating sound.

Poor Arthur picked himself up painfully and with difficulty. The closet was just wide enough for him to turn round in, and no more ; not a crack of light penetrated into the recess, for even the stairs without were very dark. But such a punishment was not entirely new to Arthur ; he had been occasionally locked up, for an hour or two, in a dark room at his home. He was considerably affronted at such a punishment being laid upon him now, and at first determined to put a bold face on the matter, and show that he did not care. But he did not find it very easy to keep up his bold spirits just then, after such a terrible beating. He began to grow very hungry too, and he could hear the others laughing and talking over their dinner.

What a weary long afternoon it seemed! Arthur did not expect, to say the truth, that he should be released before the evening, but he thought he might perhaps be wanted to take part in the evening service at the Chapel, as it was a Saint's day. His spirits began to rise a little ; surely Master Gyles could not do without the Golden Treble then !

But no such luck was his. He had nothing by which to measure the time ; but at last he heard the clattering steps of the other boys, as they left the house. They were gone to Evensong, and he was left behind.

It seemed an age before they returned. He could hear their merry voices in the hall below, and the stern tones of Gyles, as he now and then called them to order. Then it became quiet again, and Arthur knew they were learning their tasks. A sort of sickening despair came over him as he thought of his part. He felt sure he could never learn it now. Perhaps he would be let off.

Tramp, tramp, tramp ! there were the boys coming up to bed. Arthur felt very hopeless and forsaken now, but he determined to put on a

defiant spirit, that they might not think he cared.
So he began to stamp up and down in his narrow
prison, and withal to chant as loud as he could,
that they might hear him.

"Ha, listen to Vain Delight!" cried Philip's
voice outside ; and then the voice came quite close
to the keyhole, and shouted,

> "' Whosoever it hears,
> It cleaveth to his ears,
> It melteth him to tears
> As he goes thereby.'"

"Where 's thy little bird, sweet lady and
queen ?

> "' Ha, it goeth, my sweeting,
> With flyting and fleeting,'
> And I have borne such a beating—
> Alack and woe is me!"

Arthur knew that was Radford's wit.

"How goeth the part now ? how much more
hast thou learnt ?" inquired Ethridge.

"How does the verse go on that begins,
' The sea is sweet and green ? '" cried another.

"Ho, noble queen," shouted a fourth, knocking
against the door, "canst thou hear, Vain Delight ?
I will tell thee what : we had manchet and
marchpane for supper for St. Andrew's Day."

"Open the door to a houseless wanderer," was the cry of another; but then Gyles must have called, for the shouting ceased, and there was a hasty scuffle as they turned into the dormitory, the last of the troop tapping Arthur's prison door, with, "Good-night and happy dreams!"

Unkind as their merriment was, the sound of their voices had given Arthur a momentary feeling of relief, and his loneliness seemed tenfold increased when they were gone. He would not give way, however, but went on singing; first his old hunting carol—but that reminded him of home and happier days, and made his throat feel choky; so he left off, and began chanting a psalm. If he had thought about what he was singing, the good words might have comforted him in his unhappiness and solitude; but he was only shouting them in a careless, defiant, hardened mood, which was wrong, and of course did him no good. Indeed, such treatment as poor little Arthur met with was very likely to harden him.

He stopped singing at last from sheer fatigue. The poor little Golden Treble sounded very strange and hollow and muffled in the dark closet, and when the boys were all in the dormitory they could not hear him. He knew it must be late at night now, it was all so still. Then by degrees all his spirits, real or put on, seemed to forsake him; and into the mind of the lonely, weary, frightened child darted a sudden thought of terror—perhaps Master Gyles was going to leave him there *for ever!*

It might be so. Arthur had heard of people being walled up in houses to starve, and it might never be discovered or known what became of them till hundreds of years after, when their skeletons were found in the wall. Oh, if this were to be his fate! Arthur, if he had considered, might have seen that this was very unlikely; Master Gyles would certainly have no object in murdering him: on the contrary, it was for his interest to take care of the Golden Treble; but a child, alone and frightened, does not reason. He got thoroughly possessed with this idea, and as each moment went by it gained force.

Poor Arthur's hair seemed to stand on end, and a cold perspiration covered his body as he thought. He was sick and faint with hunger now, but what would it be by-and-by? He wondered if he should feel himself turning into a skeleton. And then he went on to picture to himself what the people who found him would think, what they would say. He had almost grown amused with that idea, but when his thoughts came back to the reality it made him shudder the more. He called and shouted. Perhaps somebody might hear him, and come to see what it was. He called each and all of his companions by name. If Etheridge, if Radford, if Philip even opened the door, how welcome would any teasing be ! Oh, if William Byrd would but come in ! And at last, in an agony of fear and despair, the poor child fell sobbing on his face on the floor, crying aloud between his sobs, " Mother, mother ! " though he knew—knew only too well—that that mother was far away, and never even guessed what her child was suffering.

Another terror presently beset him. Arthur, like most little boys of that age and this, believed implicitly in ghosts ; especially as in those days, as I have said before, people were much more given to credit the marvellous and the supernatural. Of course, so the poor child thought to himself, there had been other victims buried in the wall, before now ; and that in some form or other they would appear to him, seemed the likely and natural conclusion. And he could not even cover his face with his hands ! He pressed his head against the ground with his eyes tightly closed, too frightened now for tears.

Poor Arthur did not go the right way to comfort himself. He had grown careless and irregular during the last year, especially since Byrd left, about his prayers, and he had lost some of his simple faith and conscientiousness, some of his manly courage too. In his lonely misery, as he lay calling upon those who either could not or would not hear him, he remembered not the Presence of One with Whom the darkness is no darkness, ever watching over him, ever able and ready to hear his cry and to help him. While he was shutting his eyes, peopling the darkness with images of terror, he did not think of the bright pure guardian spirits, really around him, though he saw them not. If he had brought such truths to his recollection, he would surely never have worked himself up into such an agony of fear.

He cried himself to sleep at last, in that uncomfortable position, on the bare floor. He was thoroughly tired out, but his sleep could scarcely be called rest, for the painful and confused dreams which troubled it—the images of his miserable waking thoughts made real. So passed the

I

night ; and it seemed to him endless, in spite of a tolerably long time of unconsciousness.

Oh, the horror of waking in that stifling darkness to recollection of his position ! His wakefulness told him it must be morning, but not a crack of light did it bring. He heard movements in the house, the voices, the steps of his companions : then they clattered down-stairs. He hoped they might call to him as they passed—even a mocking joke would have been better than nothing ; but no, they hurried down without appearing to remember him, and his horrible suspicion was confirmed. He tried to call, but seemed to have no power of uttering a sound. At last he heard footsteps approaching once more— those of a single man ; it must be Master Gyles. His heart beat so that he could scarcely hear ; the steps came nearer and nearer ; then—they stopped at the door, and—yes, the key was put into the lock, turned, and . . . a sudden rush of fresh air and light, and Arthur was conscious of no more, for he fell plump down before Master Gyles in a dead faint.

When he came to himself he was in the hall, and the first thing of which he was sensible was Master Gyles shaking him, telling him to look up and eat some bread and meat, while all the other

boys were crowding round, looking at him in a
mixture of curiosity and amusement. They
had never seen such a thing before ; and not a
few insulting remarks were passed on the paleness
of Vain Delight. They were not quite without
pity, however. When Arthur was at length able
to sit up and look at the food, Etheridge and
Morley came and sat down on either side of him,
and pressed him to eat. In a very short time
he had recovered himself sufficiently to devour
the bread and meat with much satisfaction.
It was such an untold relief to find that Master
Gyles did not intend to starve him to a skeleton
after all, that he did not seem to care for teasing,
lessons, or anything else.

But Master Gyles did not consider that the
loss of the hawk was by any means expiated.
Arthur was allowed to dine with the rest, and to
stay down-stairs to learn his tasks ; then he had
another though less severe flogging, and was
marshalled off to the dark closet again for the
night. However, the dark closet had lost half
its terrors. Arthur was not easily frightened for
nothing : he managed to sleep tolerably well that
night, and did not faint when unlocked the next
morning.

This treatment was continued for three days,

at the end of which time Master Gyles thought
sufficient impression had been made upon the
luckless boy ; and as there was to be a rehearsal
of the play, he wanted Arthur to be bright and
lively. Moreover, Master Tallis had inquired
one morning, after service, what had become of
the Golden Treble.

The rehearsal was looked forward to with
some excitement by the boys ; but it proved a
scrambling interrupted affair. Arthur, who had,
wonderful to relate, repeated his song perfectly
in the morning to his master, relapsed into
Gluttony's verses when he came to rehearse in
earnest. Gyles' anger and the blows which
accompanied it scared the rest of his part out of
Arthur's head ; and his hesitation, mistakes, and
confusion caused extreme merriment among his
fellow-actors, who seemed disposed to get up-
roarious. Sapience went into fits of laughter
at the original and impromptu sallies of Gluttony :
Life and Discretion quarrelled, because both could
not speak at once : Youth gave a sly pinch to any
of his colleagues who unfortunately came in his
way ; and Death sat chuckling and making
grimaces at the rest from a corner of the stage
till his momentous part began. The stage
direction ordered that " Here shall Death chase

Vain Delight about the stage and off ; " but Vain
Delight had no notion of ignominious flight.   On
the contrary, she turned round in an attitude
decidedly pugnacious, and, when menaced by the
dart of Death, replied by a pretty severe blow.
Indeed poor Arthur was so bewildered, so tormented by the behaviour of his companions,
that he was in no state of mind to distinguish
acting from earnest.   The performance was
abruptly terminated by Master Gyles stepping
on to the stage, parting the combatants, and
administering the rod to the most unruly.

But it would take too long to recount the
attempts, the failures, the fights, and the floggings
which were the daily, almost hourly, scenes
at Master Gyles', while " The Pilgrimage of
Pleasure " was in course of preparation.   Suffice
it to say, that at length, after many weary hours to
master and pupils, a more respectable rehearsal
was accomplished, and there was some hope that
the actors would know their parts perfectly by
the appointed time.   Arthur had mastered his,
song and all, and had contrived to get through it
without breaking down ; he was quite set up in
consequence.

" Ah ! yes, it 's all very well to crow now,"
said Philip maliciously, when the last rehearsal

was well over. " Wait till thou hast donned thy ruff and thy farthingale, and then see how much of the part sticks in thy head ! "

" Oh, that won't make any difference."

" Won't it ? Just you see! It 's all the difference in the world, when one is in his every-day garments, or dressed up like a woman. And if you break down the night of the play, you know, ah ! I would not tell thee for something what will become of thee ! "

" Oh, what, what ? " cried Arthur, in mingled curiosity and alarm.

" Ah ! " and Philip looked very mysterious, and was provokingly silent. Arthur went on teasing to be told, till at last he said, " Wilt thou know ? well, then," and he lowered his voice to a confidential whisper, " once upon a time, there was a boy here, about your own age, who never *could* learn aught by heart, just like you, you know," added Philip with great relish. " Well, he had a part to act with a great many lines in it, and he got it, as he thought, quite perfect, but when he came to be dressed and go on the stage, he forgot it all, and broke down in the middle."

" Well, well ? " said Arthur impatiently.

" And the master was so wroth with him—

but thou wilt not care to know the rest, I trow."

"Yes, yes, tell me. What did the master do?"

Philip spoke in a low voice, and with due emphasis: "He put out his eyes—with a red-hot iron."

Poor Arthur opened his own great brown eyes to their full extent with horror, and his countenance fell to a degree extremely gratifying to the narrator. "Oh, Philip, I cannot—you will make me break down; I cannot act——"

"Aha! look out for thyself," was all Philip's consolation.

"But Master Gyles couldn't put my eyes out; I'm sure Her Majesty, and Master Tallis, and all of them, wouldn't let him; I couldn't read the prycke song, you know," Arthur went on, as though it were a point to be argued then and there. Besides which, his reason began to doubt the story.

"Oh, but it's an offence against the State, you know, to break down, if you play before the Queen. It's law."

Arthur had no means of contradicting this.

"Philip," he asked presently, in a low awe-struck voice; "did you see the boy?"

"See him? of course I did."

"After his eyes were put out?"

" I told you I saw him."

" What did he look like ? "

" Look like ? why, of course, he looked like—
he looked like a boy."

" But his eyes ? "

" Of course they looked like eyes—till they
were put out, I mean."

" But after they were put out ? " persisted
Arthur, with a boyish attraction towards details
of horror.

" After they were put out ? why, of course,
one didn't see them ; one only saw the holes."

" Did he make a great screaming ? "

" Thou hadst best go to them who did it, to
know that. 'Twas not I."

The arrival of supper put an end to this
enlivening conversation, but it may be guessed
whether Arthur thought of anything else during
the whole evening. His dreams, too, were
haunted by what he had heard ; and he alternately
fancied that he was vainly trying to remember
his part, and that Gyles was standing over him
with a red-hot iron.

Next day was the eventful one : the play was
to take place in the evening. When the other
boys were allowed to go out for a time to amuse
themselves, and to freshen up their spirits, Gyles,

who was extremely anxious that Arthur should
get through his part well, bade him remain at
home, and look over it carefully. The hawk
had not been recaptured. Master Gyles did not
know whether he should be able to procure one
for the evening : but had he done so, he would
not have left it in Arthur's care.

Poor Arthur sat alone, feeling very miserable.
All the pleasure and amusement he might have
felt in the acting was gone. He only thought that
everyone was against him, and he should be sure
to break down ; and Philip's terrible story sat
like a weight upon his spirits. How he wished
that Her Majesty would change her mind, and
not, as she intended, honour the children's
revels with her presence ! He turned over the
leaves of the book listlessly. The words were
very firm in his memory now ; but when the
ruff and the farthingale were put on, and all the
audience were looking at him, where would they be ?

A footstep in the passage made him look up ;
and then the door was opened, and William
Byrd's head was thrust in.

" Is Master Gyles within ? "

Arthur started up with a sudden feeling of
relief and protection. " Oh, Will, is 't thou ?
Master Gyles is not here ; come in."

" I have brought home a truant," said Byrd,
smiling as he entered, and now drew forth his hand
from under his cloak. Upon it sat the hawk—
Vain Delight's very hawk, which had caused its
luckless owner so much grief. " I marked it,
flying low amongst the houses, as I was leaving
the Chapel but an hour ago. I watched it, for I
thought it could be no other than yours : and
after a while, it perched on a low roof, not much
above my head. I waited awhile, and called it,
as I have seen men use to do when hawking, and
it flew down and perched upon my hand. It is
tame now ; it wants food."

" Oh, Will, I am so glad ! Yes, it is of a surety
our hawk ; I know that bar in his tail. I will
find him some meat."

" And how gets on the part ? " continued Byrd,
looking into Arthur's open book.

" I think I know it now," answered Arthur,
" but I 'm so afraid—Will," he said, suddenly
lowering his voice, " if I break down, will they
put my eyes out ? "

" What ? " said Byrd, in a tone of great
amazement, turning round upon him.

" Philip said once there was a boy broke down,
and the master—he didn't say if it was Gyles—
put out his eyes with a red-hot iron. Philip says

it 's law, and they 'll do it to me, and——" here
poor Arthur's voice became very tremulous, and
he burst into tears.

Byrd's face flushed up to his forehead with
indignation. " So this is what he has been
telling you, to help you in your learning ! If I
may but catch him once——"

" Isn't it true, then ? " said Arthur, looking
up with his piteous earnest eyes.

" True ! it 's as true a lie as ever was spoken ! "
cried Byrd. " Never you believe a word that
comes out of the mouth of that scoundrel. I
cannot think how you could believe this, Arthur ;
you must surely have known——"

" He told me it was law, when I said Her
Majesty and Master Tallis wouldn't let them.
He said it was an offence against the State to
break down before Her Majesty."

" Offence against the State, quotha ! " said
Byrd, with an indignant snort. " He 'll offend
against the State some day, if he goes on as he
hath begun ! "

" Then, wasn't it true about the boy breaking
down ? "

" A boy did break down once, some years
back, in a soliloquy. I can remember that. It
was before Gyles came. Old Master Bower—he

was not so infirm as he is now—used to take all
the charge then. The boy had a flogging, but
that was all. He was an idle fellow, and had taken
no pains to learn, so it served him right. As to
offence against the State, it 's no more that than
if ye sang a false note in Chapel, or I chanced to
draw the loud stop when I would have the soft.
So put it all out of thy credulous silly head,
Arthur, boy."

"I am so glad! I am so glad!" repeated
Arthur. "I shall not be afraid now. And
Master Gyles will be well pleased to have the
hawk. Listen! they are coming in."

And into the hall burst Philip, Radford, and
Morley. Without a word, Byrd pounced upon the
former, collared him, and boxed his ears soundly.

"Take that, and that, for a great cowardly
liar! So, thou must use thy precious wits to coin
tales wherewith to frighten thy youngers and
betters! Take that!"

"Oh! let go! I didn't mean to frighten him!"
cried Philip, kicking and struggling in Byrd's
powerful grasp. "I didn't think he 'd be such
a blockhead."

"Didst not?" said Byrd, redoubling his
energy. "Perhaps thou takest me for blockhead
enough to believe thee now. Take that, then,

for adding lie to lie !" and with a last and tremendous cuff, Byrd let him go.

Philip walked away and sulked.

"And now fare ye well, gentlemen of the Chapel !" said Byrd, who, having exhausted his indignation on Philip, had quite recovered his usual good humour. "I shall see a transformation to-night ! Good luck to thee, Mistress Vain Delight," he added, clapping Arthur on the back. "See that thou have the hawk in safe keeping !" and away he ran.

Arthur did not mind Byrd calling him Vain Delight. His spirits had risen wonderfully in the last half-hour. He was too happy in the safety of his eyes to care even for Philip's angry look, and the muttered threats that he would "teach him to go telling tales to Will Byrd."

CHAPTER V

A FEW hours later in that same day found the whole company in the bustle and excitement of dressing for the play.

Arthur began by enjoying the fun, but long before Vain Delight's toilet was completed he was heartily tired of it. Besides, he thought it was beneath his dignity to be amused with it ; and there was much certainly that was disagreeable in the process. Let any schoolboy of twelve think what he should feel at being arrayed by several officials, both male and female, in the complete court dress of a lady of his own time, and he will have some idea of what Arthur suffered at the hands of barber and tirewoman. And it must be remembered that a court dress in those days was even more elaborate, and far more uncomfortable than one in the present fashion.

The barber's task was an especially tedious one to Arthur. All his glossy curls had to be tightly combed and dragged off his forehead, and fastened up, as we see in pictures of Queen Elizabeth. Above this structure of hair came the crown of " rubies fair," and " good gold "—not so good or so fair perhaps as the song might warrant, but answering their purpose very well. The barber was cross, and provoked with Arthur for not sitting still, and so hindering him. As he had to operate upon the heads of Pleasure, Sapience, and Discretion, there might be some excuse for the rough manner in which he dealt with Vain Delight's tangled locks ; and the cuffs which he administered to her from time to time.

The tirewoman was more compassionate. She was won by Arthur's bright eyes and droll ways : nay, she felt some pity for him, as he winced and fidgeted under the infliction of the hard tight corsage, and the stiff prickly ruff. Arthur, won by her kindness, grew quite chatty and communicative ; and by the time his toilet was finished, he had melted her almost to tears with the recital of some of his misadventures. Then she kissed him, and pronounced him to make the sweetest little lady that ever was seen ; which Arthur considered an insult, and if it had not been so very long since he had known anything like a woman's tenderness

he would have been angry. As it was, he sub-
mitted passively.

Then Master Gyles tramped into the room to
see how his company were getting on.

"Ha!" he said surveying Arthur, "the
character suits him well enough, but his cheeks are
too pale. A little rouge would methinks be an
improvement."

Now, Arthur was naturally, as we have said, of
a ruddy complexion, but London life, and of late
hard treatment and the dark closet, had com-
bined to rob him of his fresh colour. Poor little
Vain Delight could certainly not have boasted of
being ruddy just then.

The rouge-pot was produced. Philip and Morley, released from the barber's clutches, rushed up
to see and ridicule. "Ha, dainty lady, hast thou
lost thy roses? Mind she doesn't faint. Oh, see
her beauty!"

"How the grand ladies will admire him!"

Those taunts brought some real colour not only
into the cheeks but over the brow of poor Arthur ;
but he was forced to submit to the ignominious
process of painting. At last it was finished, and
he was set free.

But now that he was ready, and the awful
moment drew near, the dread of forgetting his

part and breaking down returned, though the consequences were not so dreadful as he had once believed. To fail before the Queen and the Court, let alone the gentlemen of the Chapel, who knew him so well, was sufficiently awful.

"Do hear me say my song, Morley," he said plaintively, "I won't be long ; I'm so afraid."

"Do go thy ways with thy whining," was the answer ; "dost thou think nobody has a part but thyself ? "

"Radford, wilt thou, then ? "

"Nay, surely ; thou art infected with too many of my rhymes already," replied that worthy personage, Gluttony, folding his hands and looking down serenely upon the unwonted rotundity of his form.

"Etheridge——" began the poor boy in his despair, running from one to the other.

"Don't 'Etheridge' me," answered he, turning round a death's-head mask upon him, "I can't be plagued with thy song, forsooth."

So one and all met him with a rebuff, till Gyles called out, "Arthur Savile, it would be well that I should hear thy song the last thing. Repeat."

Arthur, thankful for the chance, began,

"I am mickle of might,
I am seemly of sight,"

K

and so on, with rapid but monotonous utterance,
till he arrived at the sixth verse—

> " The sea is full sweet and green,
> Thereas no wind hath been ;
> I am lady and queen,
> Both by sea and by land ; "

but having proceeded thus far, he continued, with
the utmost gravity and unconsciousness,

> " I am a full fat swag,
> I shake as doth a bag,
> As I go my sides sag,
> Unnethes [1] may I stand."

Imagine the fury of Thomas Gyles ! Forgetting everything in his rage with the hapless boy,
he cuffed Vain Delight till the fabric of hair, the
crown, and the flowers, came down in ruins. It
was the old, old mistake ; Gyles had hoped that
the floggings and the dark closet had eradicated
it ; but to-night, of all times, it was come back,
and the effect of Gluttony's lines, pronounced in
the simplest manner by the ruffed and stately Vain
Delight, with her earnest tearful eyes, and plaintive monotone, was irresistibly comic. The other
players were in a wild state of merriment. Master
Gyles would have stripped and whipped him then

[1] Uneasily.

and there; but time pressed, and there was the barber's work to do again. He paused for a moment almost in despair.

"This addle-brained fool will never do to go on the stage; he will spoil the whole affair. I must seek Master Bower, and ask his counsel. In the mean while," he turned to the rest, "hold yourselves in readiness. And ye," addressing the barber and tirewoman, "do up the knave's hair as ye best may."

He departed. Arthur, who had only just awakened to a sense of his delinquency, looked from one to the other in bewilderment. "What is he going to do? Who is Master Bower?"

"Master Bower, knave? Dost not know who Master Bower is?" said Philip.

"No. Oh, now I bethink me Will Byrd said Master Bower was master a long while ago, when the boy broke down. Is he living yet?"

"Don't come to me to know that," was Philip's reply; "thou wilt not believe me, thou knowest."

"Oh yes; tell me."

"Well, then, Master Bower is the master over and above Gyles. He never takes much account of the boys, because he is old and infirm; but when he does—— Ah, I would not be in thy shoes for something!" Philip shrugged his shoulders.

K 2

Etheridge and some of the younger boys pricked up their ears in some apprehension.

" But how is it we never see him ?   Does he go to Chapel ? "

" Surely, sometimes.   Thou canst not see him because thy side is Cantoris.   But *I've* seen him look at thee," added Philip, with a knowing wink and shake of his head.

" No, but now, is it true ? "

" True ?   Doubt Gyles' word, if thou wilt."

" But what will he do to one ? "

" Ask thy friend, Will Byrd, since he is the only fellow worthy of thy credit."

" When did he look at me, Philip ? "

" When ?   Oh, I'm sure I cannot call to mind ; scores of times.   I've seen him," continued Philip, perceiving that his auditors were growing credulous, " I've seen him watch thee awhile, and then lean forward and whisper to another, ay, and shake his head.   Look thou, Etheridge, that thou knowest thy part, for he may call on thee, as the last comer.   I've known mine for the last fortnight, thank goodness ! " drawing himself up proudly, and looking immensely pleased with himself, in his " ash-colour satin doublet, laced with gold lace," and " cloth of silver hose with satin and silver panes,"—a sumptuous dress, truly.

" Oh, do somebody hear me say my part first ! "
pleaded poor Arthur with tears in his eyes.

" A likely thing, in sooth," was the utmost he
could get from any of them, and Philip strutted
away. The rest hung about him during the
second infliction of the barber, who was exceedingly
put out at having to dress his hair a second time,
and made him suffer accordingly.

Poor Arthur became more and more nervous
and frightened, with a real tangible alarm to
which the vague terrors of the dark closet and
Philip's story seemed as nothing. He had been
living under a delusion, believing that Gyles was
the head master, that in knowing him at least he
knew the worst : whereas all this time there
lurked above and behind a supreme, awful, though
hidden power, of whom Gyles was but the agent.
It would be difficult to describe the terror with
which the poor boy was inspired by the idea of
" old Master Bower."

His distress moved the heart of the sympathizing tirewoman, who kissed him again and again,
to the extreme mirth and disdain of Philip and the
rest, telling him that no one would hurt him, only
he must not cry, or he would spoil all his paint !
He tried hard to choke his sobs, but in vain ; and
the barber boxed his ears and pulled his hair worse

than ever. Certainly "The Pilgrimage of Pleasure" had brought little pleasure as yet to poor Arthur.

At length, just as the cross barber had put the finishing touch to his headgear, steps were heard without—a heavy, measured tread. Was the terrible Master Bower coming? The boys gathered together in subdued expectation.

The door opened, and enter Master Gyles, in company with an elderly man of grave countenance, dressed in a style that had been the prime of the fashion some years back, but was now becoming a little antiquated. His hair and beard were white, the latter short and square, unlike the peaked form of beard that was then generally worn. On his head was a little black cap, and he leant upon a staff. His aspect was imposing, and to Arthur was sufficiently awful.

But " old Master Bower " was not altogether so old or so infirm as the boys were wont to imagine ; and the slight concern shown by him in the active part of their management, was owing as much to his dignity as to his age. He had been Master of the children of the Royal Chapel under the Kings Henry VIII and Edward VI, and was continued in that office by the Queen, with a salary of forty pounds a year, upon which he lived very comfortably and at his ease, troubling his head but little about the every-day details of the establishment, which he left almost entirely to the supervision of his energetic subordinate, Gyles. Perhaps the terror which he inspired might be attributable to the fact that it was only in extreme cases, such as the present, that this functionary appealed to him.

Poor Arthur, with his bewildered face, on which tears and rouge disputed for the mastery, presented a pitiful appearance, in spite of his brave attire. " You may see how it is, Master Bower," Gyles said, as he pointed to him. " For the last three weeks and more hath it been my labour, by day and by night, to teach that knave his part : and if thou wilt believe me, his brains are now in that confusion, I dare not adventure him on the stage. I am fairly at my wits' end."

Master Bower fixed a pair of keen searching eyes upon the unhappy child. " Boy ! " he said, sternly, " how is it that I hear this ? "

Arthur could not, if he would, have spoken.

" Perhaps, Master Bower, you would hear him repeat a portion of his song. You may then judge whether he be fit to appear."

And, to Arthur's terror, Gyles handed the book to his superior. " Now, boy, speak ! " he said.

For the hundredth time he began the song of

Vain Delight, but in low mournful tones. Master Bower rapped with his staff on the ground impatiently. " Speak up, knave. How shall an audience hear thee, if thou mumble thus ? "

Arthur raised his voice a little ; but his manner was painfully timid and hesitating. No wonder : the poor child scarcely knew what he was saying, and was each moment in dread of a sudden blow. But he had just sense enough left to watch himself in the sixth verse, and went through it without borrowing from Gluttony.

" He hath the words correctly," said Master Bower, when he ended. " The manner is bad. Are the rest of the company perfect ? "

" I can answer for them," replied Gyles, with confidence. " Philip Drew, come forward, and let the Master hear how thy part begins."

Philip obeyed, reciting his opening lines with a promptitude and clearness of pronunciation which pleased the old man, who was a little deaf, and liked people to speak plain and loud. He commended him much. " The boy hath a good presence and a distinct utterance. Let me advise ye, boys, to take pattern by your senior player. And thou," turning to Arthur with a warning look, " take heed to thyself, or thou shalt not be spared."

" I sometimes think with myself whether I am

not over-lenient with the knave," said Gyles, as the old master turned to depart. " None can believe the pains I have been at with him from first to last ; yet I do assure you, Master Bower, the more I flog him, the less he seems to repay me. It is a thankless office, in sooth!" This last was a sort of aside, as he followed Master Bower out of the room.

Arthur remained standing in vague apprehension, wondering if the worst were past, or something yet more terrible lurked behind : while the tirewoman, as she put the last finishing touches to his dress, told him, in sympathizing and tender tones, that he need fear nothing : he had said his part to perfection, and a sweet and a pretty part it was ; not a word but what was truth, either. If he were not fair and bright and goodly, she would like to see who was ! and with that she embraced him, and was rewarded by having his ruff poked into her face. She might mean to be very kind, but she little knew the shame and the teasing that she was bringing upon him.

But it is time to introduce our readers to the theatre upon which Arthur was now to make his *début*. The stage arrangements of those early days were very poor and simple compared with those which we see now—though England was such a play-acting country. There were no painted shifting scenes, and in consequence a great deal was left to the imagination of the spectators, who were requested to believe this and that— much as children at play imagine themselves in a ship, or in a house, or in a carriage, without any real change of place. The stage was a raised platform at one end of the room : upon it, towards the rear, was a balcony or upper stage, probably supported by pillars, and about eight or nine feet from the ground. From hence, in some of our old plays, part of the dialogue was spoken ; in front of it were hung curtains which occasionally concealed the persons who were upon it from the audience. This supplementary stage, however, was not requisite for the representation of the interlude for which the children of the Chapel were now preparing.

On the evening in question, a goodly company had assembled in the theatre to witness " The Pilgrimage of Pleasure." There sat the stately Queen herself, conspicuous in her ruff and gorgeous dress of purple cloth of gold, blazing with jewels and gold ornaments. About and around her were the ladies and great lords of the court. The rest of the theatre was filled with spectators of various ranks. On the stage itself, where critics and judges of the performance were at that time allowed to sit, old Master Bower had taken up his position, to supervise the acting of his boy-subjects. Thomas Gyles, as active manager, was here and there and everywhere, gathering his troop together, priming, admonishing, scolding, as the occasion might require.

And now the eyes of the spectators were turned towards the stage, where Morley, in the character of Pleasure, was about to speak the Prologue. He was dressed as a woman, in a black velvet gown embroidered with gold lace, and being a slim fair boy, he looked well enough. He was not new to the stage, and was very composed and unabashed, as he spoke :

" All children of men, give good heed unto me,
    That am of my kind very virtue bodily.
    Turn ye from following of lies and Vain Delight
    That avaunteth herself there she hath but little
        right :
    Set your hearts upon goodly things that I shall
        you show,
    For the end of her ways is death and very woe."

After a little more good advice in the same strain, Pleasure's part was over until the Epilogue, and she retired—an object of extreme envy to her unfortunate rival, Vain Delight. Youth and

Sapience then went upon the stage, " disputing as thus," (it was Youth who spoke first) :

" Away from me, thou Sapience, thou noddy,
    thou green fool !
What ween ye I be as a little child in school ?
Ye are as an old crone that moweth by a fire,
A bob with a chestnut is all thine heart's desire.
I am in mine habit like to Bacchus the high god,
I reck not a rush of thy rede nor of thy rod."

The pride and contempt with which Philip Drew, in his " ash-colour satin doublet," pronounced the last sentence, may be imagined. He was in particularly high feather that evening, being immensely set up by Master Bower's commendation.

Then Life entered, personified by Thomas Fleming—a good-looking, ruddy boy, in a white satin doublet faced with red taffety. He proceeded to give sage counsel to Youth, after the following manner :

" Bethink thee, good Youth, and take Sapience to
    thy wife,
For but a little while hath a man delight of Life.
I am as a flame that lighteth thee one hour ;
She hath fruit enow, I have but a fleeting
    flower ; "

and so on, while Youth appeared to give but little

heed to his counsel. After which Sapience departed from Youth, and Life was supposed to cast him into a deep slumber, and so left him " for a space." While this is going on, we must take a glance behind the scenes for a few moments, where Vain Delight, whose part follows, was standing passively while Thomas Gyles was tying the hawk to his wrist.

Arthur was beyond tears now. He had swallowed them down, and had received a fresh coat of paint, under which his poor little face was twitching nervously.

" Now, knave," said Gyles, when the bird was securely fastened, " how doth thy part begin ? "

Arthur looked round, with his piteous, searching eyes. " My name is Vain Delight," he uttered after a moment's thought.

Gyles stamped. Only that elaborate headdress saved Arthur from a tremendous blow. It would not do to render him unpresentable at the last moment. Gyles repeated the first stanza, declared that if Arthur broke down now it would not be *his* fault, bade him look to his part if he valued his life, and drove him upon the stage.

Arthur did not seem to see or to feel all the eyes that were upon him—and they were many. He was not afraid of the Queen, before whom he so often sang, and with whom he was rather a favourite ; nor of the court or the spectators generally. All his fears were of the stern white-headed old man who sat on one side of the stage in calm dignity, and the even more stern lynx-eyed under-master lurking behind, listening anxiously for the smallest shadow of a failure.

There was some applause when he appeared. The Queen clapped her hands softly, and the example was followed by those around. They were won by his appearance, before he spoke—and, to say the truth, Arthur made a very pretty Vain Delight, the more so as he was quite un-thinking of his appearance. His dress was green, embroidered with gold, with violet silk linings ; and the quaint headdress and ruff set off his bright eyes and small regular features to great advantage. And when he was fairly on the stage, out of reach for the moment of Master Gyles, he felt a little more at his ease, and began his song right.

Wonderful to relate, he got through it safely—with the exception of forgetting to unfasten the hawk at the right moment, and sending it flying off in a great hurry, while he was in the midst of the last verse. Then Vain Delight plucked Youth by the sleeve to waken him, and he rose to follow her, and they went off the stage together.

Sapience and Discretion then appeared, the latter personified by a dark-haired lad of fourteen, in a murrey-coloured gown branched with silver, and a stiff simple headdress. She bewailed the folly of Youth in these words :

" For pity of Youth I may weep withouten measure,
    That is gone a great way as pilgrim after Pleasure,
    For her (most noble queen) shall he never have
        in sight,
    Who is bounden all about with bonds of Vain
        Delight.
    That false fiend to follow in field he is full fain,
    For love of her sweet mouth he shall bide most
        bitter pain.
    The sweeter she singeth, the lesser is her trust,
    She will him bring full low to deadly days and
        dust."

After a little more, the two grave counsellors departed together—and enter something that produced a general laugh, from the stately Queen herself to the youngest citizen in the twopenny seats : something as broad as it was long, looking like a large walking ball, surmounted by the merry rosy face of Johnny Radford, his eyes twinkling and his whole countenance brimming over with fun at his own transformation, and his comic part of " Gluttony, the Vice." A jolly good-natured looking Vice he made, as he began repeating with infinite relish the following address to his audience :

" Ow, I am so full of flesh my skin goeth nigh to
    crack !
  I would not for a pound I bore my body on my
    back.
  I wis ye wot well what manner of man am I ;
  One of ye help me to a saddle by and bye.
  I am waxen over-big, for I floter on my feet ;
  I would I had here a piece of beef, a worthy meat.
  I have been a blubberling this two-and-forty year,
  And yet for all this I live and make good cheer."

There was one among all those spectators who had not laughed even during the speech of Gluttony, which was longer than the extract we have given here. There was one pair of eyes that had followed Vain Delight, without ever leaving her, till she quitted the stage—that remained fixedly watching for her to re-appear, with a wistful seeking look. Arthur would scarcely have acted his part so steadily if he had known that those eyes were upon him.

Although he had got through his song fairly, it by no means satisfied his masters. Gyles shook him for forgetting the hawk, and old Master Bower came behind the scenes to say that he *must* speak out, and have more spirit and animation—he was making nothing of his part. Between the two, the poor child got into such an agony of nervous terror that it seemed doubtful whether he would be able to go on with it at all, though the next scene was one which he liked best, for in it he had to enter leading Youth in a bridle, typifying Vain Delight's ascendancy over him. And Youth, with perfect coolness, was strutting about the little room where they had to wait, ready bridled, making unkind jokes and taunts at the expense of his " sweet life and lady."

This was going on during the above-quoted speech of Gluttony. Poor little Arthur took the bridle in cold trembling hands, and stood repeating the first lines of his coming part over to himself. He had one instinct left—to keep them in his memory.

Master Bower took him by the hand. " The silly knave is all of a tremor," he said, and ordered Master Gyles to give him some spiced wine. It seemed a wonderful and unheard-of kindness, and when he had swallowed the contents of the glass that Gyles put into his hand, he looked up into the face of the old master with a touching expression of gratitude. He did feel a little revived now, and more able to go upon the stage,

L

though Youth gave him a spiteful pinch and bade him not faint.

But that little kindness of Master Bower had given him confidence—not but that he took it for far more than it was worth. Had not the credit of Master Bower and his assistant been staked upon the due and becoming performance of the play, it was little spiced wine that Arthur would have got from either of them. Be that as it may, Arthur thought he had never tasted anything so good in his life ; and he was in better heart than he had been as yet, as he stumped upon the stage with his bridled companion, patting tall Philip upon the shoulder, and saying coaxingly :

" I wot ye will not bite upon my snaffle, good
    Youth ;
  Ye go full smoothly now, ye amble well for-
    sooth."

  To which Youth replied :

" My sweet life and lady, my love and mine heart's
    lief,
  One kiss of your fair sweet mouth it slayeth all
    men's grief.
  One sight of your goodly eyes it bringeth all men
    ease :—"

" Ow, I would I had a manchet or a piece of
    cheese ! "

That was Gluttony's method of calling the new-comer's attention to his portly presence. Vain Delight turned towards him, saying :

" Lo, where lurketh a lurden [1] that is kinsman
    of mine ;
Ho, Gluttony, I wis ye are drunken without
    wine."

Then a banquet was set out in tempting display, to which the three jovial companions sat down ; and here Gluttony sang the song which had made such an unfortunate impression upon Arthur.

In an ancient record of the expenses of the Revels in the reign of Queen Elizabeth, we find among the charges for sundry expenses, payments to the grocer for " divers parcels of his wares," for sugar, for " rose water, gum tragachant, almonds, quinces preserved, walnuts ready made, cloves to stick in the pears, pears ready made of marchpane stuff, &c.," by which we may form some idea of the kind of feasts held upon the stage. The pears, preserves, and almonds were doubtless as attractive to the boys in their own persons as to the palates of Youth, Vain Delight, and Gluttony. On the present occasion, neither of them could refrain from partaking substantially

[1] Lout, lubber.

of the good things spread before them ; Gluttony however recollecting himself sufficiently to fall asleep, as his part required, before the entrance of Sapience and Discretion.   These virtuous and strong-minded characters were here, according to stage directions, required to " beat Vain Delight and take away her crown," requirements which they executed with conscientious pleasure, inflict-ing many pulls and wrenches upon Vain Delight's much-enduring hair, and so rendering it the easier for her to follow out the direction to " weep and wring her hands."   Thus they went off the stage.

By this time the Allegory was being worked onwards to its close.   Before the next entrance of. Youth, Gluttony, and Vain Delight, a lapse of time was supposed to have passed, and Youth speaks rather wearily :

" We have gone by many lands, and many
      grievous ways,
   And yet have we not found this Pleasure all these
      days.
   Sometimes a lightening all about her have we
      seen,
   A glittering of her garments among the fieldes
      green ;
   Sometimes the waving of her hair that is right
      sweet,
   A lifting of her eyelids, or a shining of her feet,

Or either in sleeping or in waking have we heard
A rustling of raiment or a whispering of a word,
Or a noise of pleasant water running over a
 waste place,
Yet have I not beheld her, nor known her very
 face."

Vain Delight here interrupts him with the
indignant question :

" What, thou very knave, and how reckonest thou
 of me ? "

Youth answers sadly :

" Nay, though thou be goodly, I trow thou art
 not she."

Vain Delight replies :

" I would that thou wert hanged in a halter by
 the neck.
From my face to my feet there is neither flaw
 nor fleck,
There is none happy man but he that sips and
 clips
My goodly stately body and the love upon my
 lips.
Great kings have worshipped me, and served
 me on their knees,
Yet for thy sake, I wis, have I set light by these."

Poor Vain Delight began her lines bravely
enough, but when it came to praising herself so

openly, and she saw Youth's real mocking smile behind his assumed disgust, and thought how he would quiz and tease afterwards, she blushed through all her rouge, twisted her hands, and dropped her voice. Master Bower rapped with his staff, and muttered, " Speak up." Those who were near the stage could see the little actor's nervous start, as he raised his voice again and spoke hurriedly :

" What pratest thou of Pleasure ? I wot well
    it am I."

" Ow ! I would I had a marchpane or a plover
    in a pie ! "

ejaculated Gluttony, as if thoroughly weary with the pilgrimage on which his companions had dragged him. He continued :

" What needeth a man look far for that is near at
    hand ?
What needeth him ear [1] the sea, or fish upon dry
    land ?
For whether it be flesh, or whether it be fish,
Lo, it lurketh full lowly in a little dish."

As may be supposed, this created great laughter amongst the audience, as did most of Gluttony's speeches. Indeed, Radford, of all the boys, performed his part the best, taking an intense

           [1] Plough, till.

delight in it, and having besides a considerable turn for comic acting.

Next came in Sapience and Discretion, the former speaking thus :

" I charge thee, O thou Youth, thou repent thee
    on this tide,
  For but an hour or twain shall thy life and thou
    abide ;
  Turn thee, I say, yea turn thee, before it be the
    night,
  Take thine heart in thine hand, and slay thy
    Vain Delight,
  Before thy soul and body in sudden and sunder
    be rent."

Youth answered :

" Nay, though I be well weary, yet will I not repent,
Nor will I slay my love ; lo, this is all in brief."

Thus encouraged, Vain Delight exclaimed :

" I beseech thee now begone, thou ragged hood,
    thou thief !
  Wherefore snuffest thou so, like one smelling of
    mustard ? "

" Ow, methinks I could eat a goodly quaking
    custard,"

interrupted Gluttony, and was rebuked by Youth :

" Peace, thou paunch, I pray ; thou sayest ever
    the same."

Vain Delight continued to insult Sapience :

" Lo, her coats be all bemired ! this is a goodly
        dame,
    She pranceth with her chin up, as one that is full
        nice : "

but here the persisting Gluttony again broke in :

" Ow, I would I had a pear with a pretty point of
        spice,
    A comfit with a caudle is a comfortable meat ;
    A cony is the best beast of all that run on feet.
    I love well butter'd ale, I would I had one drop ;
    I pray thee, Mistress Sapience, hast thou never
        a sugar sop ? "

Mistress Sapience, however, turned a disdain-
ful shoulder upon him with—

" Depart from me, thou sturdy swine, thou hast
        no part in me ! "

and the disconsolate Gluttony, exclaiming,

" Ow, I wist well there was little fair fellowship
        in thee,"

turned to Discretion, saying,

" Good Mistress Discretion, ye be both lief and fair,
    Of thy dish, I pray thee, some scrapings thou
        me spare."

He met, however, with this stern rebuke :

" My dish, thou foolish beast, for thy mouth it is
    not meet ;
I feed on gracious thought, and on prayer that
    is most sweet,
I eat of good desires, I drink good words for wine ;
Thou art fed on husks of death among the
    snouts of swine ;
My drink is clear contemplation, I feed on fasting
    hours,
I commune with the most high stars, and all the
    noble flowers,
With all the days and nights, and with love that
    is their queen."

" Ow, of this communication it recks me never a
    bean ! "

was Gluttony's scornful answer.

" Shall one drink the night for wine, and feed
    upon the dawn ?
Yet had I rather have in hand a cantle of brawn."

    Again Sapience urged Youth to repent :

" O Youth, wilt thou not turn thee, and follow
    that is right ? "

    " Nay," replies Youth,

" While I have my living I forsake not Vain
    Delight,"

adding, however,

" Till when my hairs are grey, I put her away
    from me."

" Nay, but in that day will I withdraw my face
from thee,"

exclaimed Vain Delight indignantly ; then, turning
to Sapience with great contempt,

" Out, out, mother mumble, thou art both rotten
and raw."

Gluttony added :

" I will reach thee, if I may, a buffet with my
paw,"

giving the buffet at the same time with such a
ludicrous effect as to call down a burst of applause.
He then with Vain Delight drove out the two
wise personages, Sapience and Discretion : Vain
Delight thus addressing the former :

" What, wilt thou take my kingdom ? have this
for all thy pains ; "

and Gluttony's comment being,

" Ow, I would I had a toast to butter with thy
brains."

There was much laughing during this scene,
over which the actors became greatly excited.

When they were gone Life returned, but in a
different garb, "an old coat, and lean and halting,"
his face being chalked to look pale. In a sad
and admonitory tone he spoke as follows :

" Lo, this is the last time that ever we twain shall
    meet,
  I am lean of my body and feeble of my feet ;
  My goodly beauty is barren, fruit shall it never
    bear,
  But thorns and bitter ashes that are cast upon
    mine hair ;
  My glory is all gone, and my good time over-
    past,
  Seeing all my beauty cometh to one colour at
    the last,
  A deadly dying colour of a faded face.
  I say to thee, repent thee ; thou hast but little
    space."

    Youth then asks :

" What manner of man art thou ? It seems thou
  hast seen some strife."

    Life answers :

" I am thy body's shadow, and the likeness of thy
  life,
  The sorrowful similitude of all thy sorrow and
    sin ;
  Wherefore, I pray thee, open all thine heart
    and let me in,
  Lest, if thou shut out good counsel, thou be
    thyself shut out——"

    In the midst of this solemn address the
audience were again moved to laughter, for here

Vain Delight and Gluttony return from their
chase ; the latter panting, puffing, and holding
his sides, the former with a very red cheek and
ear, the effect probably of a warning from a
severer hand than that of Sapience or Discretion.
In fact, he had just had a rebuff for romping and
forgetting that he was a lady, thus endangering
his gorgeous apparel. Gluttony began first to
lament himself, and boast at the same time :

" Ow, though I be lusty I have made them low to
    lout,
  My lungs be broken in twain with running over
    fast,
  With beating of their bodies mine own sides
    have I brast ;
  The heaving of mine heart it is a galling grief.
  Ow, what makes thee so lean and wan ? (*to Life*)
    I trow thou lackest beef."

  Vain Delight was getting excited. The spiced
wine might have something to do with it ; at any
rate, it was exhilarating to think that he was nearly
at the end of his part, safely through the most
trying scenes. So he turned really quite fiercely
upon the unhappy-looking Life :

      " How, what is this knave, trow ? "

and on Youth answering,

      " He saith his name is Life,"

Vain Delight went on ;

" By the faith of my fair body I will give him grief
    to wife !
    In his lips there is no blood, in his throat there
        is no breath.
    Call ye this Life, by my hood ? I think it be
        liker Death."

    Life replied :

" It is thou, thou cursed witch, hast bereft me of
        mine ease,
    That I gasp with my lips and halt upon my
        knees."

This altercation was interrupted by the sudden
and awful appearance of Death " with a dart."
It was Etheridge, grim and ghastly in his mask
and skeleton facings over a black suit. He was
a tall slim boy, and looked the part well : but
it was his first appearance on the stage, and he
had a great many lines to repeat. In spite of
his good memory he felt a little nervous, and his
tones were rather timid as he began :

" Thou hast lived overlong without taking thought
        for me ;
    Lo, here is now an end of thy Vain Delight and
        thee.
    Thou that wert gluttonous shalt eat the dust for
        bread,

Thou that wearest gold shalt wear grass above
thine head ;
Thou that wert full big shalt be shrunken to a span,
Thou shalt be a loathly worm that wert a lordly
man.
Thou that madest thy bed of silk shalt have a
bed of mould,
Thou whom furs have covered shalt be clad upon
with cold,
Thou that lovedst honey, with gall shalt thou
be fed,
Thou that wert alive shalt presently be dead."

Youth fell on his knees, crying,

" O strong Death, be merciful ! I quake with
dread of thee."

" Nay," answers the stern messenger :

" Thou hast dwelt long with Life : now shalt thou
sleep with me."

This pathetic scene was enlivened by the
by-play of Gluttony, whose expression of fear
and ungainly movements were irresistibly laugh-
able, as he cried :

" Ow, ow, for very fear my flesh doth melt and
dwindle,
My sides and my shanks be leaner than a spindle;
Now foul fall his fingers that wound up the
thread ;

Good Master Death, do me no hurt ; I wis I am
but dead."

Here Gluttony also fell on his knees, amidst the
applause and laughter of the spectators. And
that wicked little Vain Delight, who ought at least
then to have shown some terror, stood laughing
too, as Gluttony, after crying most lamentably,

" Now may I drink my sobs, and chew upon my
sighs,
And feed my foolish body with the fallings of
mine eyes,"

rolled over upon his back, struck by the dart of
Death.

" Here," said the stage directions, " shall Death
chase Vain Delight across the stage." Her part
ended as follows :

" Mine eyes are turned to tears, my fair mouth
filled with moan,
My cheeks are ashen colour, I grovel and I groan,
My love is turned to loathing, my day to a weary
night,
Now I wot I am not Pleasure, I am but Vain
Delight ! "

Her run across the stage was too much of a
dodging affair, and the audience laughed. It
was enough to make them do so, to see the quaint
figure of Death so earnestly chasing the little

lively boy—for a thorough boy he looked in spite of all his female finery—with his jumping dodging movements. Both had got into the fun of the thing, and seemed disposed to prolong the scene, encouraged by the smiling faces of the spectators, without regard to the effect. It did not signify that Etheridge chuckled behind his mask, but Vain Delight's triumphant boldness was but too apparent, as she laughed up into the very face of that grim skeleton, and jumped round and round the stage, where Gluttony was reposing a prone and lifeless lump, till by a mischance she tripped over her petticoat, and came down on her knees involuntarily. She picked herself up nimbly, and turning round caught the eyes of Will Byrd amongst the spectators, twinkling with sympathetic fun. It put the finish to Arthur's audacity. Shaking his hand at Byrd, he gave his concluding sentence, "I am but Vain Delight!" with a triumphant laughing shout that rang through the theatre, and scampered off the stage, careless of his rent farthingale, with a hop, skip, and a jump ; not quick enough however to escape a sharp crack across the shoulders from the staff of old Master Bower.

His part was over now as far as regarded the

play. We will follow Youth and Death for a while. Youth, still kneeling and cowering, spoke :

" O Death, show pity upon me, and spare me for
    a space."

Death answered :

" Nay, thou hast far to go ; rise up, uncover thy
    face."

Youth. " O Death, abide for a little, but till it be
    the night."

Death. " Nay, thy day is done ; look up, there
    is no light."

Here the candles near the stage were snuffed, darkening it considerably. It was one of the best scenes, but Philip, correctly as he could learn his part, had very little animation, and Etheridge was getting more and more nervous at the thought of some long lines that he would presently have to repeat alone.

Youth pleaded :

" O Death, forbear me yet till an hour be over and
    done."

Death answered :

" Thine hour is over and wasted ; behold, there
    is no more sun ! "

Youth. " Nay, Death, but I repent me."

M

" Here have thou this and hold,"

said Death, striking him ; and Youth, falling,
exclaimed :

" O Death, thou art keen and bitter, thine hands
are wonder-cold ! "

Death. " Fare forth now without word, ye have
tarried over measure."

Youth. " Alas, that ever I went on Pilgrimage of
Pleasure,
And wist not what she was ; now am I the
wearier wight.
Lo, this is the end of all, this cometh of Vain
Delight ! "

And with this moral conclusion to his story,
Youth, again struck by Death, fell back upon
the stage by the side of Gluttony.

Poor Etheridge, whose most formidable part
was yet to come, stood for a moment hesitating and
fidgeting with his dart. It was all very well to laugh
at Arthur, but there was such a thing as being over-
confident. Master Bower rapped once, twice.
Death went as near as he could to the prompter,
and began in timid tones, muffled behind his mask :

" O foolish people ! O ye that rejoice for a three
days' breath,
Lift up your eyes unto me, lest ye perish :
behold, I am Death ! "

Here Master Bower rapped again. He could not hear.

" When your hearts are exalted with laughter, and
    kindled with love as with fire,
Neither look ye before ye nor after, but feed
    and are filled with desire.
Lo, without trumpets I come : without ushers
    I follow behind :
And the voice of the strong men is dumb ; and
    the eyes of the wise men are blind."

Here was heard in the distance, behind the scenes, a dismal sound of crying. It was none other than the voice of hapless Vain Delight, who had escaped from the darts of Death only to fall into the clutches of Thomas Gyles, and was now paying the penalty of his romping spirits, and expiating the damage done to his farthingale, under the rod. Poor little Vain Delight ! He had hoped, as he gave that last triumphant admission that he " was not Pleasure," that the worst was over ; but no. No sooner was he off the stage than Gyles seized him, in vindictive fury, to visit upon him the anxiety and trouble that the whole night's affair had cost himself.

Etheridge heard, and knew the sounds only too well ; and the probability that a like fate awaited himself if he failed did not help him now. If anybody could have looked behind that ghastly Death's head, they would have seen a face almost as pale, and pitiful in its troubled expression. He stammered and paused; and then suddenly remembering himself, gabbled on, as if repeating a lesson :

" Your mouths were hot with meat, your lips were
      sweet with wine,
There was gold upon your feet, on your heads
      was gold most fine :
For blasts of wind and rain ye shook not neither
      shrunk,
Ye were clothèd with man's pain, with man's
      blood ye were drunk ;
Little heed ye had of tears and poor men's sighs,
In your glory ye were glad, and ye glittered with
      your eyes.
Ye said each man in his heart, ' I shall live and
      see good days.'
Lo, as mire and clay thou art, even as mire on
      weary ways.
Ye said each man, ' I am fair, lo, my life in me
      stands fast.'
Turn ye, weep and rend your hair ; what
      abideth at the last ?
For behold ye are all made bare, and your glory
      is over and past.
Ye were covered with fatness and sleep ; ye
      wallow'd to left and to right.

Now may ye wallow and weep : day is gone,
    and behold it is night !
With grief were all ye gotten, to bale were all
    ye born,
Ye are all as red leaves rotten, or as the beaten
    corn.
What will one of you say ? Had ye eyes and
    would not see ?
Had ye harps and would not play ? Yet shall
    ye play for me.
Had ye ears and would not hear ? Had ye feet
    and would not go ?
Had ye wits and would not fear ? Had ye seed
    and would not sow ?
Had ye hands and would not wring ? Had ye
    wheels and would not spin ?
Had ye lips and would not sing ? Was there no
    song found therein ?
A bitter, a bitter thing there is comen upon you
    for sin.
Alas ! your kingdom and lands ! alas ! your
    men and their might !
Alas ! the strength of your hands and the days
    of your Vain Delight !
Alas ! the words that were spoken, sweet words
    on a pleasant tongue !
Alas ! your harps that are broken, the harps that
    were carven and strung !
Alas ! the light in your eyes, the gold in your
    golden hair !
Alas ! your sayings wise, and the goodly things
    ye were !

Alas! your glory! alas! the sound of your
names among men!
Behold, it is come to pass, ye shall sleep and
arise not again.
Dust shall fall on your face, and dust shall hang
on your hair;
Ye shall sleep without shifting of place, and shall
be no more as ye were;
Ye shall never open your mouth; ye shall never
lift up your head;
Ye shall look not to north or to south; life is
done, and behold, ye are dead!
With your hand ye shall not threat; with your
throat ye shall not sing.
Yea, ye that are living yet, ye shall each be a
grievous thing.
Ye shall each fare under ground, ye shall lose
both speech and breath;
Without sight ye shall see, without sound ye shall
hear, and shall know I am Death."

Etheridge's long part was over, and he
drew a deep breath. They did not applaud
him much, and he was rather disappointed
as he turned away, after this considerable
feat of memory, if nothing else. The howl-
ings in the background, too, had done much
to shake his composure.

A scene of wrath and terror awaited him at
the back of the stage, and the cause of the noise

which had penetrated to the theatre was soon discernible. Vain Delight, stripped of her farthingale and held by Sapience and Discretion, was yet undergoing the penalties of the law at the hand of the enraged master. It was a sad end to " The Pilgrimage of Pleasure " !

" I wot I will turn his eyes to tears, and his mouth to moaning ! " Gyles was saying. ": Turning his part to jest and buffoonery, and tearing a new dress with his antics ! I trow I will give him somewhat to jump for ! " and again the rod descended with redoubled force.

Master Bower, however, who had followed Etheridge off the stage, here interposed, saying that the noise was audible in the theatre, " though for a word this mumbling knave," pointing to Death, " spoke, it mattered little. I have seldom heard a speech worse delivered," he added, " and I would that his back felt the taste of the rod, Gyles, while there be a twig left."

Gyles had paused in his work, and now turned to the trembling Etheridge, who began to whine and whimper behind his mask in pitiful tones. " Oh, good Master Gyles—oh, sir, I did not break down ! " and then subsided into speechless tears. All in vain. He was divested of his death-like trappings, and delivered over to the hands of

justice—or injustice, as he most undoubtedly
considered them.

But we must once more return to the stage,
where Pleasure stands to speak the Epilogue. He
had been sitting at the back of the platform, in
happy unconcern, watching the actors both before
and behind the stage ; and now he went forward
again, fresh and bright and unabashed as before.
It was a relief to hear his easy clear recitation,
after Etheridge's monotonous utterance.

> " The ending of Youth and of Vain Delight
>   Full plainly here ye all have seen ;
> Wherefore I pray you day and night,
>   While winter is wan and summer is green,
> Ye keep the end hereof in sight,
>   Lest in that end ye gather teen ;
> And all this goodly Christmas light,
>   Ye praise and magnify our Queen,
>   Whiles that your lips have breath ;
> And all your life-days out of measure,
> Serve her with heart's and body's treasure,
> And pray GOD give her praise and pleasure,
>   Both of her life and death."

The Epilogue brought great applause, and
Morley bowed and walked out. It was over now,
"The Pilgrimage of Pleasure "! and sore pains
and trouble it had caused to actors and managers.
It is to be hoped at least that the audience were

edified, and that so all the pains and trouble had not been quite thrown away.

Etheridge's punishment was in process as Morley returned from the stage. Sapience and Discretion yet acted as supporters to the unhappy victim, who, divested of all attributes of Death save his skull, presented a somewhat grotesque appearance. Vain Delight, in a disordered toilet, was sobbing apart, subject to the insulting comments of Youth; while Gluttony, in supreme contentment and immunity from disgrace, sat calmly surveying the scene. In the midst of it all, Master Bower returned, to say that the audience were calling for the players. They had better all come upon the stage.

Master Bower's will was law. Gyles laid down his rod, bade Death attire himself again, fastened up Vain Delight's farthingale as well as he could, gave her a shake and a cuff by way of stopping her tears, and marshalled his troop upon the little platform once more.

There was a great deal of applause as they appeared : some sympathizing smiles, too, at the sight of poor Vain Delight's tearful face. Death was better off, for that grim mask concealed his woeful countenance. There were one or two hearty laughs as the audience welcomed their

old friend Gluttony, restored to life and serenity :
there were curious admiring glances at the goodly
dress of Youth, the sweeping skirts and stately
forms of Sapience and Discretion ; and there was
one low cry, like a woman's stifled scream, but it
was scarcely heard in the crowd and the movement
of departing spectators.

The lights were extinguished one by one as
the players retired. As they went behind the
stage, a porter accosted Master Gyles. " A
gentleman without demanded to speak with him."

Master Gyles bade his boys wait, and went out.
Presently he returned. " Arthur Savile, follow
me ! "

Arthur looked up, and obeyed with trembling.
The events of that day and night had been almost
too much for him, alternating between fear and
pain and excitement : he had only a dull sense left
of something to dread—though what, he did not
know.

Gyles led the way along a dark passage to a
door of a little room which he opened, and then
pushed Arthur forward.   There was a light, and
several persons were in the room—whom, Arthur
had no time to see, for there was an eager glad
cry, a pair of arms were thrown around him, and
he was clasped to his mother's breast.

It was like a dream. Arthur could not believe
that it was true, but his one instinct was to
cling to her, regardless of his ruff and headdress,
till a voice behind him said, " Well, boy, hast
thou never a word for thy father ? "

He turned round at that, and met his father
with an eager though less impulsive greeting.
Parents and children were more formal in their
intercourse then than now. Master Savile laid
his hand upon Arthur's shoulder. " I scarce
know thee, boy," he said, surveying Vain Delight's
tumbled finery with a half-puzzled expression :
" look me in the face, that I may see if thou be
indeed my son Arthur."

Arthur looked up with his ready smile. In the
sound of the familiar home-voices he forgot his
troubles.

" Yes, yes, I see—it is thou thyself," said
Master Savile, and he gravely kissed his son's forehead ; " thou art grown somewhat, and hast lost a
little of thy colour and sturdiness. But I would
fain see thee in thine own clothes."

" And I would fain that he put off these, while
two rags of them hold together," put in Master
Gyles : " come, knave, thou hast done enough
damage to our stage properties to-night. Come ! "

Arthur hung back, but his father said, " Go,

Arthur; Master Gyles will allow you to return to us."

So Arthur went, and in a few moments was arrayed in his own clothes; and very thankful he was to get rid of the impediment of his farthingale, and the stiff tight bodice, which galled him sadly. He received a rebuff for pulling and tearing the few of Vain Delight's remaining flowers out of his hair, but at last they were all safely extricated, and his curls fell down in their wonted manner again, only very rough and tangled after their hard usage.

Himself once more, he was returning to his parents, when in the passage he met Will Byrd, amongst some other visitors to the theatre who were departing. He instantly seized him.

" Here are come my father and mother, Will! and you must come and see them! Sir," addressing his father, as he entered the room, " this is my friend Will Byrd, and he saved my life and picked me out of the river ! "

Honest Will blushed on being dragged into the presence of a strange lady and gentleman by the impetuous little boy. Master Savile, however, shook him by the hand, saying that if such were the case they owed him a great deal ; and Mistress Savile embraced Arthur again, with tears. " But,

child," she said, " why did you not come home,
when you were picked up out of the river ? "

" Oh, it was not our river," replied Arthur.
" It was in a boat on the Thames—we were upset."

Here was a sad puzzle for poor Mistress Savile !
Arthur, too, began to recollect that the adventure
was altogether not one to boast of, especially in
the presence of Master Gyles.

Arthur's parents entreated to be allowed to
take him that night to the inn where they lodged.
Gyles hesitated and demurred, but finally gave
a grudging permission, on condition that he
returned the next day.

So Arthur went with them, and heard all that
they had to tell. How they had been so firmly
persuaded that he was drowned that they had
given up all hope, and had taken no further steps
than searching in the river. How Master Savile
had come up now on business .to London, and
brought his wife with him : how he had persuaded
her to go to the play, as she had never yet been out,
or been to see anything, since they lost their
child : how she had been struck by the first sight
of Vain Delight, and had watched, and clung to
the bare possibility, and scarcely dared to believe
her eyes, though she did not think they could
deceive her in this ; and how, when he laughed

and uttered his last triumphant shout, she had
doubted no longer, but felt quite, quite sure that
Vain Delight was no other than her own lost
Arthur. All this was quickly told; and then
there was Arthur's story to be heard. His
mother was very much distressed when she learnt
that he was taken from them so unkindly and for
so long; and asked Arthur how it had happened,
when he could write, that he had never written to
let her hear that he was alive. Arthur replied,
with tears, that he had once begged permission to
do so, but that Gyles had sternly refused him.
This was the truth. In fact, Gyles, so long as he
did his duty by Her Majesty's Chapel, did not feel
answerable to the relatives of the children whom
he impressed into her service. His meeting with
Arthur had been a fortunate chance, at a time
when he was expecting shortly to have a vacancy
in the choir on account of Byrd's leaving it. He
had carried him off hurriedly, congratulating
himself on avoiding a " scene " of any kind. If
the parents of the child cared to come and look
after him, it was all very smooth; he knew how to
answer them. If not, so much the better: he
would let well alone, and not go out of his way
to look for them. If he was exceeding his commission by this piece of needless tyranny, he did

not feel any compunction on that score. He had supplied the choir with a first-rate treble before a deficiency could be felt ; and he left the rest to chance, deeming that he might shelter himself, if accused, in the inferiority of his position.

Arthur had, besides, many questions to ask about his sisters Lucy and Katherine, and his brother, little Will, who had remained behind at Ferryton. And by degrees, too, he told of many of his own troubles—though they seemed nothing to look back to, now that he had found his parents. It made his mother unhappy when he told her about Gyles' severity, and the unfortunate affair of the hawk ; but owing to the strict and harsh notions regarding the management of children which prevailed in England then, she was perhaps not so much shocked or surprised as a mother might be nowadays in such a case.

Arthur's father went himself to Master Gyles with him the next day, and made a formal request to that functionary that Arthur might be permitted to return with them into the country for a time at least. Gyles looked very glum at the proposal ; in fact, he was not pleased at the unexpected appearance of Arthur's parents : partly, it might be, from a secret consciousness that he had acted with unwarrantable injustice towards them.

He was very nearly making a flat refusal then and there; but he did not dare go so far as this. So he answered, evasively, that he had not sufficient authority to give the permission; intending in his heart to take no further measures to procure that authority.

Arthur, however, confided his hopes and wishes to his ever-sympathizing friend, William Byrd—he was so afraid Master Gyles would not let him go home. Byrd spoke a word in his favour in the ear of his master, Tallis; and Master Tallis consequently exerted his influence with the authorities. The event was that Masters Bower and Gyles, after laying their heads together, consented to spare the Golden Treble to visit his parents in the country, for the space of three weeks, when the Christmas Services and festivities should have come to an end, on condition that he should return punctually to a day at the conclusion of the time specified or, if he was wanted, sooner.

So one bright frosty morning, early in the new year, a small travelling party might be seen on the road leading from London in the direction of Ferryton: Master Savile, with his wife behind him on a pillion, on one horse, on another their serving-man, and behind him, Arthur. It was a different ride, indeed, from his last along this road.

And what a happy meeting was there, when at length they arrived at the old Grange ! How Arthur's little sisters kissed and hugged him, as if they would devour him ! And little Will, who was so much grown in the two years that Arthur declared he should not have known him if he had met him in the street, only his face was just the same !

But it would take too long to tell of all the rambles and rides and snowballing and skating that Arthur contrived to get into those happy three weeks which he spent at home ; or the quiet peaceful Sundays when, as of old, he joined the village choir, whose " plain-song " seemed very " plain " to him after the music of the Chapel Royal, where Tallis' beautiful harmonies to the Morning and Evening Services had lately been introduced. He often took part, too, in glees and carols at home, with his parents and sisters ; little Will joining with a heartiness and tunefulness that gave promise of his becoming one day a second Golden Treble.

The happy time came to an end only too soon, as happy times always do. Master Savile was a conscientious man and a loyal subject. He regarded his son as a servant of the Queen, and therefore, when the appointed day arrived, he sent Arthur with the trusty serving-man off to London ;

not however without previously giving him much good advice, and warning him against evil company and example.

I will not say that Arthur did not cry when the time came to bid farewell to his happy home and his dear mother, or that his heart did not sink within him at the thought of returning to Master Gyles. He put a brave face on the matter, however, promised to remember all that his parents told him, to speak the truth, and to be diligent in his work. And when he arrived at Master Gyles', he was looking quite bright and happy.

A change had taken place in that establishment during his absence. Philip Drew, his prime tormentor, had left, having lost his voice, and Radford, merry good-natured teasing Radford, was the senior boy. His headship proved a far pleasanter and less tyrannical one than that of his predecessor, as Arthur found. Morley, the next in age to Radford, was a quiet studious boy, with a great turn for music, in which he resembled William Byrd. Etheridge, who had been disposed to follow Philip's lead in bullying his juniors, was comparatively inoffensive now that the baneful influence was withdrawn ; and altogether Arthur's third year in Her Majesty's choir was a happier one than the two which preceded it, although his innate heedlessness not unfrequently led him into scrapes, and Master Gyles was by no means disposed to be more lenient with his faults as time went on—in particular, with the inaptitude which he always showed for learning by heart.

I wish I could say that all the plays acted by the Children of the Chapels Royal were as innocent and instructive as "The Pilgrimage of Pleasure." The "Moralities" might be very well in their way, but I fear that many of the pieces which in those times were publicly performed by children were such as no child would nowadays be suffered to read. True, the ideas and manners of the sixteenth century were very different from those of our own ; but it is very sad to think of the young hearts and lips of those who were especially set apart to lead the Services of the Church being so early made familiar with wickedness. At any rate, we should be very thankful that our lot has been cast in happier times, when so much more thought and pains are given to teaching the young what is right and good, and keeping them from evil, than was the case in days gone by.

And now, having followed Arthur's career thus far, we must say what remains to be said of him in brief. He remained at Master Gyles' three years after Philip left; at the end of which period the Golden Treble followed the fate of all trebles, and he was of no further use in the choir. He was not however entirely cast off by those whom he had served for so long, but was placed at Eton by the Queen's appointment, to continue his education. Although he was then past the age at which boys can now be admitted scholars there, it is doubtful whether the same law was in force in those days ; but that, if it were, it has been over-ruled by Royal authority is nearly certain.

In the same year that Arthur left London for Eton, William Byrd was appointed organist of Lincoln Cathedral, which post he held for six years. But Arthur never forgot his early protector, and their friendship lasted through life, in spite of the difference between the characters and pursuits of the two friends. Arthur, although he never proved famous for application, and made perhaps as frequent acquaintance with the birch as any Eton scholar before or since, acquitted himself with fair credit at school : he also continued to take great delight in the practice of music, though having little head for its theory. His after-life was prosperous, though not altogether uneventful. When he was about thirty-five, he joined the campaign that was then being fought in the Netherlands, in which his career, though short, was honourable. After this he returned home, married, and lived long and happily.

His successor at Gyles', when he left, was no other than his brother, little Will, then a fair slim boy of ten, looking less able to cope with the severities of that master's establishment than Arthur had been, but in reality standing a better chance from his greater docility and steadiness. Our friend Gyles went on and prospered : later in life he became Master of the boys of St. Paul's school, with full Royal authority for taking up from time to time " apt and meete children " to be instructed in music and singing, which authority no doubt he continued to exercise with his wonted unscrupulousness. It is to be hoped, for the sake of the boys and the master too, that they proved " apter and meeter " in learning their tasks than did poor Arthur over "The Pilgrimage of Pleasure."

The name of Byrd, whose story has been interwoven with that of our hero, has become famous among those of our native musical composers. Of his private life we know little, but that little may lead us to infer that he was an amiable and a religious man ; the former from the testimony of his contemporaries and friends, his master and pupils, among whom was numbered Thomas Morley: the latter from the constancy with which he dedicated his talent to Church Music.

He died at a good old age in 1623, having survived his venerable and beloved master Tallis thirty-eight years. He has left behind him a large collection of musical compositions, both sacred and secular; and among his " Eight Reasons for Learning to Sing " is a saying well worthy of preservation, which might fitly become the motto of every chorister, old and young: " The better the voice is, the meeter it is to honour and serve GOD therewith : and the voice of man is chiefly to be employed to that end."

THE END

Glossary

p. 7: *plain-songs*: a form of vocal music used by the Christian church since the earliest times. It later came to refer to a simple melody or theme, often accompanied by a running melody or descant.

p. 21: *pryck-songs*: music sung from notes written or "pricked," as distinguished from that sung from memory or by ear. The phrase refers to written vocal music.

p. 71: *catspaw*: a person used as a tool by another to accomplish a purpose.

p. 73: *wherry*: a light rowing boat used on rivers to carry passengers and goods.

p. 109: *manchet*: a small loaf or roll of the finest wheaten bread.

marchpane: a confectionery composed of a paste of pounded almonds, sugar, etc., and made up into small cakes molded into ornamental forms.

p. 126: *tirewoman*: a lady's maid.

p. 132: *cantoris*: pertaining to a cantor or precentor; applied to that side (north) of the choir of a cathedral or church on which the precentor sits.

p. 152: *comfit*: a confection consisting of a piece of fruit, root, or seed preserved and coated with sugar.

caudle: a drink usually consisting of warm ale or wine, often mixed with bread or gruel, eggs, sugar, and spices.

Note on the Text

Between 1864 and 1910 *The Children of the Chapel* went through three editions. The first edition was brought out in 1864 and the second in 1875. Both were published by Joseph Masters and Co. of London and the title pages of the first two editions are almost identical, including the exclusion of Swinburne's name. The third edition was published in 1910, a year after Swinburne's death, by Chatto and Windus of London. Its title page does acknowledge Swinburne's presence, or at least some of it, in the novel: *The Children of the Chapel* / By Mrs. Disney Leith / Including *The Pilgrimage of Pleasure* / A Morality Play by / Algernon Charles Swinburne.

It was in the Preface to the third edition that Swinburne's cousin described in some detail the nature of their collaboration. Because of the historical and literary interest of this Preface, I have based this edition upon the third edition. Except for minor stylistic and grammatical changes and corrections, however, the three editions are virtually identical. I have retained the original spelling, punctuation, and grammar. I have also included a brief glossary of some of the archaic words and expressions found in the novel.

Robert E. Lougy